Chapter

A pale skinned, white haired woman picks berries from a bush on the side of a woodland trail, her long hair tied into a plait down the left hand side of her face. She brushes a stray strand away from her eyes with the back of her hand. Arella stands from her bending position, taller now than she used to be. She has grown into a beautiful strong woman, independent and fierce. Arella has become adept at hunting, and with the help of Maska, can catch just about any game animal in the forest. Arella has also lost some of her clumsiness, and is now more agile than ever. She can run through the forest with ease, never tripping on the roots that tangle on the floor. Arella now knows this forest like the back of her hand. It is her home, and she has made it just that.

The forest has not changed much, although it feels smaller. Arella has lived in the forest now for four years and has investigated every inch of the land. She knows where each rock lies, where the edible berry bushes are, where each animal sleeps, everything. Her and Maska have made the forest their home, and they rule this land, or that is how it seems. Abundant food and shelter has made living rather easy, and although the winters can be hard, they have always pulled through, because they have each other.

Four years has passed since the day when Arella and Maska, with the help of a pack of wolves, defeated the small group of tribesmen who had been tormenting and cruelly killing the animals in the forest with poison arrows. She often thinks of that day, and how weak she was. If it happened again, Arella would deal with it better. She is stronger now, and would not have been so easily brought down. Maybe she would have landed the killing blow, rather than the jaws of a wolf. But she cannot change the past, only allow it to shape her future.

The sounds of gargled screams filled her dreams for weeks, haunting her. In the months that passed after that day, Arella became depressed. She felt guilty for causing the ends of their lives. Maska managed to keep her going. He kept her distracted. After a while, Arella began to see that they had to do what they did, and the fact that she was no longer seeing the animals in her forest in pain and fear helped to strengthen this. Since that day, neither Arella nor Maska fear the wolves. They have a mutual respect for them, and often pass them on the paths, both ignoring each other. Their howling no longer worries Maska, and they both enjoy the sound, knowing the wolves are close, hunting in their territory. It's comforting, knowing they're there.

With winter approaching soon, Arella is gathering berries deep in the forest. Although she has bushes close to home, she would like to save them for the dark of winter when it's too cold and snowy to venture away from her treehouse. She takes a hand full of berries and places them in her doe skin bag. Above her, a squirrel chirps. She looks up at it. "You want some?" The squirrel chirps again. Arella picks another few berries on a small stick. She holds the stick up to the squirrel. "Here you go." With her red ears twitching, and her bushy tail wagging, the squirrel takes the branch from Arella's hand. Arella is broken off from her task of berry picking by a strange sound. Familiar voices fill the air in the forest. It has been about four years since those voices have filled Arella's ears yet she cannot quite place it. She recognises the voices, but cannot picture their faces. One voice sticks out from the rest, strong and deep, but soft and musical to listen to. She knows the face of this man. Green eyes, although she cannot remember his name. Arella is anxious to see the men, to know if they came back okay or not, but she is also worried because the last time she saw them, they had seen her. She wonders what stories they will have to tell, or if any of them are scared. Arella is excited to hear them laugh again. It has been a few months since she has heard another human voice, keeping away from people if she can. Arella turns to look at Maska, but finds him already gone. The fully grown auron cat was intent on hunting today, and this is where he must have gone, leaving Arella in the forest on her own. She puts the bunch of berries she last picked into her old does skin bag and starts walking in the direction of the faint voices, butterflies in her stomach.

As Arella walks, the voices get louder and she notes that all four of the men are in this group, along with a couple of younger voices she does not recognise. She recognises one laugh in particular. She closes her eyes to hear it better. Green eyes fill the darkness behind her eyes. A smile escapes Arella and she catches herself. The butterflies in her stomach dance more the louder his laugh becomes.

This week has been particularly bright, the sun shining bright and low in the winter sky. Although the snow has not yet started, Arella knows it will not be long. With her hood shielding her eyes from the glare of the bright winter sun, Arella makes her way towards the voices.

The blotchy light coming through the dying leaves of the trees above helps to shield Arella from view as she gets herself into position to watch the men talk. They are in the same old clearing that they always used to practice in. This brings back memories for Arella. Memories of the last time she saw them, the great wolf attttempting to make them his last meal. As she looks around, she is pleasantly surprised. All four of the original men are in the clearing, although they all look older.

As Arella comes up on the clearing, she is grateful the men are all in high spirits and laughing. The noise of their laughter masks the light crunching of the autumn leaves beneath her feet. This is not a good time of the year to be stalking, nor a good time for hiding. The trees are beginning to shed their leaves, making hiding in them a lot harder. Arella resorts to hiding in a conifer bush. This has not lost any of its foliage, nor will it ever. It has grown large, and hides Arella well.

From between the branches, Arella watches with purple eyes. The first person her eyes focus in on is Nashoba, his green eyes glinting in the low sunlight, the corners turned up and watering with laughter. The features on his face have grown stronger and older, but still soft and kind. His hair has grown longer, and he wears it tied behind his head. He is wearing brown trousers made from doe skin, and is wearing a think vest. Arella wonders if he is cold in the cooling autumn air. His arms have grown bigger, and his shoulders strong. They move up and down as he laughs. "The funniest part was when Doahte fell in the river." He cracks up at the end.

"That was not funny." Doahte pouts. "It was cold." The others all laugh at him. "You wouldn't have liked it if a wolf badger atttacked you. "

"Attacked you…?" Nootau buts in. "It hardly attacked you." They all laugh, but Arella can tell it is in good spirits.

Arella is watching the expressions on Nashoba's face change as he tells the stories from their years away. She no longer hears the words, nor understands their meaning. All she can hear is the sweet sound of his voice. She shakes herself. "Get a grip girl." She thinks to herself. "This is not the time to be thinking like this. You have way to many things you need to be doing, and all of them more important than being here." Just as she thinks this, Maska appears next to her, silent as the night. He's been hunting, but looks to have come up short tonight. This doesn't happen often, and he looks a little annoyed. He nudges Arella, clearly wanting to go home. "A couple more minutes Maska." Arella whispers. "Then we will go home."

She moves her eyes away from Nashoba's face to take in the others. Nootau has not changed all that much, although his hair is now cut short. Arella wonders why this is, although sometimes men do decide to cut their hair, it is not often. She also notices the feathers in his hair. He now has several of them, five she counts, all adorning his shoulder length black hair. Nootau has chosen to start growing a beard, although it is not quite growing all over his face yet, it makes him look older. He is too wearing the doe skin clothing, but has short sleeves rather than a vest. A new tattoo also adorns Nootau's arm. It is a tribal design, although Arella does not know its meaning.

Next in the circle of people is Doahte. He has not changed at all. He is still small and scrawny, with mischief in his eyes. He makes Arella laugh, kind of funny looking, with ragged hair and ragged clothes. He always looked like this, but Arella hasn't really looked at him that closely before.

Next in the circle that Arella recognises is Mato. The first thing she notices before anything else is the scar on his face. It covers his left eye and goes down his cheek. It looks deep, but is now white and healed. Arella wonders what beast could have done that to someone as strong as him. She is sure this story will have been told already, but she would love to hear it herself. Arella then notices the size of Mato. His harm and shoulders are enormous. He has grown a lot stronger as he has gotten older. The four years that Arella has not seen the men has changed them a lot.

Children sit with then men in a circle in the woodland. There is a small fire in the middle of the clearing, and Nootau is cooking boar over the flames. The smell rises up into Arella's nostrils making her hungry. Arella notices that all of the children are boys. There is a younger woman in the mix also, she looks to be about fifteen years old, and there is something recognisable about her. Arella looks at her features, then at the other men. Her eyes are the same shape and size as Nashoba, although they are not the same hypnotising green as his. He smiles at her, clearly love in his eyes. "And while I was away..." He starts to say. "My little sister... My fifteen year old little sister, fell in love with her childhood friend." He smiles at her. Arella notices that she is holding hands with one of the other young men in the tribe. "He is soon to go on the trial we just went on, and when he comes home they will be married." This deserves a celebration I think, and I'm sure my father would have agreed." Arella wonders why Nashoba is talking about his father in the past tense. She looks over at Nashoba's sister and sees tears in her eyes. He must have died while Nashoba and the others were away. Arella feels sad for him and the others. She knows what it is like to loose someone.

Nashoba quickly turns it around. "So tomorrow night, in my fathers honour, we will have a celebration." The others in the group cheer at this, and Nashoba's little sister smiles through teary eyes, her intended husband holding her tighter for comfort.

The men and Nashoba's sister tuck into the boar from the fire and talk amongst themselves. Arella focuses on the conversation between Nashoba's sister and her intended. "Are you sure you have to go on this trip Chogan?" Nashoba's sister asks. "I'm worried you won't come back." Tears fill her eyes again. He kisses them away. "Oh sweet Nova. I will come back, and I will marry you. Don't you worry about that my butterfly." She smiles at this, reassured by his confidence. They snuggle closer to each other and the stories continue. It's sweet, watching them. From where she is, Arella can only see Chogan's face, his eyes filled with so much love It makes Arella smile. He has a nice looking face, strong features, but there is something likeable about him.

Arella is watching the expressions on Nashoba's face change as he tells the stories from their years away. She no longer hears the words, not understands their meaning. All she can hear is the sweet sound of his voice. She shakes herself. "Get a grip girl." She thinks to herself. "This is not the time to be thinking like this. You have way to many things you need to be doing, and all of them more important than being here." Just as she thinks this, Maska appears next to her, silent as the night.

Chapter 2

With the laughter fading into the background, Arella and Maska start the walk back to their camp. Maska has caught a couple of rabbits in his hunt and carries them proudly in his mouth. He'd left them a little away from Arella, before going to meet her. "So you did catch then?" Arella says, laughing at Maska. He's done this a couple of times now, making her think he's not caught, then bringing in his catch. When they are far enough away from the group to not be heard Arella talks. Maska purrs loudly, his body vibrating as he does so. "Well I hope one of those rabbits is for me." She smiles. "Because from the blood on your paws, you've already eaten." Arella pauses. "Am I right?" She nudges Maska, who now comes up to her stomach, and has strong wide shoulders. He just nudges her back, almost knocking her over as he does so. Arella laughs. "I'll take that as a yes then." She continues laughing as she walks on, Maska at her side. "I can't believe you started eating without me." She looks down at him, and he looks up at her. "Oh come on I'm joking. You can eat without me. I don't mind. As long as you bring me some back. You know that don't you?" Maska purrs In response.

As Maska and Arella walk through the forest, the familiar sights and sounds of the forest all around them. They make it back to the clearing they call home in good speed, their knowledge of the land and terrain helping them to navigate with ease. The twisting roots here no longer a problem, the land very easy to navigate when you know it as well as they do.

Stepping into the clearing where the treehouse is, Arella notes the differences in how it looks. She thinks back to four years ago when the men left for their trial, and how bad the clearing looked. The ground was all churned up from planting the bushes, and they looked scrawny and half dear, the treehouse was very viable and looked unsafe, and the chickens were completely exposed. Now, Arella can see the beauty in her home. The treehouse is almost invisible atop the three white trees, hidden by vines that hang down and tangle to the ground. The ground hut is also nicely hidden, the bushes Arella planted growing high and hiding it from view. The bushes Arella planted behind the trees have grown strong and tall. The chicken coop has also been moved and is now closer to the tree. The pen has grown, and the walls have been built higher. Arella can now walk inside the pen, bent in the middle and hunched over, but she fits inside. A roof was also put on the top of the pen, giving the chickens some cover and protection. She lost two of the chickens in the first winter, but now has a strong flock of twelve chickens and two cockerels.

The trees around the clearing have started to turn. Oranges and browns have started to show themselves and the leaves are falling from the trees. A blanket or dead leaves is starting to cover the ground in the clearing, and the leaves crunch under Maska's paws as he pads across the ground. He takes his kill over to the fire pit in the ground hut and drops them on the black stone. He looks at Arella expectantly and she smiles at him. "You can't tell me you're still hungry? How many of those rabbits did you eat before you brought them back to me? Two?" Maska shakes his head. "Three?" He shakes it again. "Four?" Maska pauses and a catty smile lights up his face. "Wow. You piggy cat." Arella laughs. She moves over to the fire pit, picking up kindling and flint. As she lights the fire, Arella thinks about the men she saw in the clearing again. There must be some reason for her seeing them. The spirits would not have led her to them again if not for a reason. The spark of the fire brings her out of this thought. Arella then prepares the rabbits and begins cooking them on a spit over the open flames. She has taken out the innards and given them to Maska, as usual, and she will share the cooked meat with the great auron cat, although the greedy beast has probably had enough for the day. "Looks like you won't need any food for the next couple of days." Arella says.

With a mouth full of cooked rabbit, Arella remembers the reason she was in the forest in the first place. She was picking more berries. These berries belong to a bush that Arella has struggled to grow herself. Taking clippings from this bush did not work, and every time she tried, they would just die. Arella's second thought was to pick the berries, remove the seeds and plant them. She needs a lot of these berries though, as she wants a lot of bushes. The berries on the manoa tree are very sweet, and full of energy. They will be perfect food when winter comes next year. Of course they will not grow for this winter, with it only a few months around the corner, but the seeds can take root at least and lie dormant in the soil while the frost and snow cover the ground.

    She gets up from her spot on the ground and moves over to the hollow in the white tree where she left the deerskin bag containing the manoa berries. Opening the bag, Arella takes the berries in her hand. She splits each purple berry open, revealing the bright pink flesh within, and the black seed within. After a while of doing this, Arella has a handful of black seeds, purple stained hands and a lot of fruit flesh on one of the black rocks. "Oh dear Maska." Arella says sarcastically. "Looks like I'm going to have to eat all of those berries tonight before they go off." Maska rolls his eyes at her and continues chewing on the rabbit leg.

    Moving over to and area of mud Arella has excavated earlier, she begins to plant the black manoa seeds, one by one, until they are all in the ground, covered with a light dusting of soil. Arella knows that some of these seeds will get eaten before they have chance to grow, but with a few dozen planted, she should end up with at least a few bushes by next year.

Arella looks down at her hands, purple and muddy. "If my hands looks like this, I dread to think what the rest of me looks like." She walks over to the lake, removing her clothing as she goes, and climbs into the cool water. Maska watches her go, then continues munching on the rabbit leg. Although he likes water, he does not like the cold. Arella however, feels refreshed when she has been for a cold bath.

Water laps at Arella's chest as she floats in the water, staring up at the sky, the sun setting and faint stars beginning to peep through the sky. The moon is rising, and the sun is falling, the end of another day.

After a while in the water, Arella feels like she is clean enough to get out. Well either that or the skin of her fingers is so wrinkled she feels like an old woman. She swims to the edge and rubs herself dry. She then puts on her clean set of clothes and washes her others. Her doeskin cloak is the only thing she does not wash. She only has the one, and would be cold without it tonight.

Arella hangs her clothes to dry and moves back over to Maska. She takes a spare cooked rabbit leg and continues eating it, eating the manoa berries with it. "I forgot how nice these tasted Maska." She says through a mouthful of food. "You really are missing out with only eating meat." He just rolls his odd coloured eyes at her and licks his paws, cleaning off the blood and grease from the rabbit.

Maska purrs as he cleans himself, a soothing sound to Arella. As well as the sound of Maska's purring, and the crackling of the fire, Arella can hear the other sounds of the night coming to life. She moves out of the cover of the ground hut and lies herself down on the cold grassy ground. With a bed of orange and brown underneath her, Arella looks up at the stars and watches them float past.

Small bats flit through the sky, twittering as they go, catching moths that are attracted to the light of Arella's fire. Maska has fallen asleep by this fire, and he snores softly. An owl hoots on a branch close by, and it too flies over Arella's head, searching for voles by the water's edge. Arella watches the owl beat its great wings, silently gliding through the sky.

No matter how long Arella lies on the ground staring up at the stars, she cannot seem to turn her brain off to go to sleep. The light of the fire is all but gone, and Maska's snores have grown louder. "At least you're sleeping." Arella whispers to herself. She gets up from the ground, brushes the leaves off her cloak and moves to inspect the chicken coop. They too are all asleep, huddled in a corner, the feathers of one another keeping them warm. Quiet cooing can be heard as they slumber.

    Moving over to the hollow in the tree, Arella takes her bow and arrows, straps them to her back and adjusts them so they are comfortable. She then takes her dagger from its safe place in the hollow and fastens it to her boot. With this done, Arella turns and sets off into the forest. Maska will not worry when he wakes without her, and if he feels she has been gone for too long, he will simply follow her trail and scent until he finds her. Arella is taking her bow and dagger as defence just In case she comes across something that would like to make her dinner, although she highly doubts this will happen. No big predators have been seen in these parts for a while now, and the wolves will leave Arella alone.

    The forest is dark, but an almost full moon lights her way. Arella walks and walks, not really paying must attention to where she is going. Soon she finds herself in a familiar place, the clearing. Arella laughs to herself and looks up at the stars. "The spirits do things for a reason right?" She asks the sky. "So I guess I'm here for a reason then." Arella brings her eyes back down to the ground.

Something shines on the floor. Arella moves over to the shiny object and picks it up. It's a necklace made from red stone, a small wolf carved into it. "Pretty." Arella admires the stone wolf, its features perfect and small. She takes the necklace and hangs it around her neck. "I wonder who it belongs to?" She asks no one in particular. "Whoever it is can't miss it that much. They just left it here for me to find." She holds it again in her hand, looking at the detail. "Well thank you to the spirits for guiding me to this."

The stone wolf sits between Arella's breasts, next to her heart. She inspects the rest of the clearing and finds the pit where the fire was, all burnt out and cold. They must have left the clearing a long time before now. The indents where they were all sitting can be easily seen. The four men, Nashoba, Nootau, Mato and Doahte, as well as Nashoba's sister, Nova, and her intended husband Chogan, and the other younger men. From the tracks on the ground, Arella thinks there were about another six people around the fire, although she cannot remember.

In the distance, faint in Arella's ears, the sounds of the party at Nashoba's tribe can be heard. She can hear the dim thumping of drums, but the other sounds are lost to the night. Arella looks to the stars, tucks the red wolf necklace under her clothes to keep is safe, then walks towards the sound. She knows the way to Nashoba's village, but she lets the drums guide her through the trees, all the while, keeping her guard up in case any of the tribe members have strayed from their village site.

The beating of the drums shakes Arella's chest. The rhythm is soothing, but joyful and energetic at the same time. Laughter can be heard before the people laughing can be seen, and the light from the many fires lighting the trees in front of her, causing them to be nothing more than black silhouettes. Arella moves carefully towards the edge of the clearing and walks along it, keeping an eye on the villagers in the glade. She finds herself a tree that still holds most of its leaves and climbs into it. Using her cloak as camouflage, Arella hides in the tree to watch the celebrations.

All members of the tribe are dressed with long feather skirts, headdresses and body paint of all different colours. Some men and women sit playing great big drums with animal skins stretched over them, creating a rhythm for the others to dance to, while others chant and sing. Arella can't help but smile as she watches this performance. It is nice to see people being happy and celebrating something. In the middle of the circle, next to a great fire pit, Arella can see Nashoba and Nova. They are dancing together, big smiles on their faces. An elder comes forwards, and the noise in the tribe quietens down. "We gather here today, under the light of an autumn moon, to celebrate both life and death." Old man Ujarak says. "While we may have lost our chief, we have gained four men. Nashoba, Nootau, Mato and Doahte came back from their trial men, deemed worthy by the elders. Now a new chief must take the place of the old one. The people have chosen Takoda." He looks over to a tall man, slight greying in his black hair, small wrinkles next to his eyes. "Until Nashoba has been trained in the ways of leading out tribe, Takoda will lead us. Let us celebrate our new chief tonight, and remember the one we lost." A few of the women, especially Nova, shed a tear, but the overwhelming feeling in the tribe is happiness. They have clearly done their grieving for the chief, and are not ready to move on with their lives.

The partying goes on for a few more hours, dancing, singing and eating. Everyone is in high spirits and not the slightest bit tired. It is only now, watching the village like this that Arella starts to get tired. Just watching everyone dance is making her sleepy. "It's a bit late to be going back home now." Arella thinks to herself. She decides she will simply stay in the tree for that night, and head back to her home in the morning. It wouldn't be the first time she slept in a tree, and most of the tribe should be up late with being up this long. That will give her plenty of time to get away without being seen in the morning.

Before Arella knows it, she is awake again. Having grown used to a comfortable bed of animal skins to sleep on, Arella is sore and uncomfortable when she wakes. She looks around, and seeing that there is no one around, she makes her way down from the tree and stretches. Her shoulder clicks as she does this, but it feels nice. Just as she is about to start her walk through the forest back to her home, Arella hears the sound of footsteps coming towards her. She looks to the village. Nashoba and Nootau are up and awake. The sun is not even up, so why are they. "Early birds." Arella sighs. This is going to make getting home without being seen a little harder. "Nevermind. I will just follow them to the clearing, then skirt around and go home. Shouldn't be too hard." She pulls herself back to hide in the bushes, using her cloak to shield herself from view. Nashoba and Nootau walk right past her and on into the forest, talking as they go.

"You sure you're okay with your sister getting married to Chogan? Don't you think she's a bit young. She's only fifteen." Nootau asks.

"Chogan is going away in the summer for his trial, then they will get married when he returns. She will be old enough to marry by then." Nashoba steps over a fallen log. "Besides, there is nothing I can do to stop it, and Chogan is a nice enough guy, just a little cocky."

Arella has to watch her step as she moves, careful not to make a sound. The dead leaves underfoot are making this hard, but thankfully they slow the pace, making it easier for Arella to follow quietly. "So why are we here again Nashoba?" Nootau asks.

"We're going hunting, just me and you." A big smile comes across his facing, reaching his green eyes.

"Hunting on our own?" Nootau scowls. "Are you sure that's a good idea?" He looks expectantly at Nashoba.

"Well why not? We can handle anything this forest can throw at us."

"So what were you planning on hunting then?"

"Something small to start I think. How about we go after boar?" Nashoba suggests.

"Boar? You're really starting us out that low?" He laughs. "We fought off great wolves and brought down bison, and you want us to go for boar?"

"To start with yes." Nashoba looks at Nootau. "Oh come on. With just the two of us, do you really want to be carrying a fully grown buffalo back to the village in the rain?"

"What rain?" Nootau says. Just as he says this, a big cold droplet of rain falls onto Arella's nose, almost making her sneeze. She catches herself, making a tiny sound.

"What was that?" Nashoba asks. He heard the sound, but could not tell where it was coming from.

"Maybe it was your White Ghost." Nootau bursts into laughter, and Arella has to stifle a giggle too.

"Oh come on. You must have gotten over this already. You know better than anyone that there was someone in the woods with us that day." Nashoba looks annoyed, but slightly amused too. He knows he was right, and so does Arella. It is like their little secret.

Even with the rain beginning to fall, Arella decides that it might be fun to watch Nootau and Nashoba hunt for boar. She knows what the boar in this area can be like, and that they are not easy to catch in the slightest. Her mind wanders briefly to Maska, but again she remembers that he is a big boy now, he can handle himself. Besides, if he needed her, he would just call out to her. His voice is the loudest in the forest, and Arella would have no problems finding him if he needed her.

After a couple of minutes walking, and not that far into the forest, Nashoba and Nootau suddenly quieten. "Shh." Nashoba says. They both stop and look around. "I can hear it in the leaves, snufflffling around. " They have been following the cloven hoof tracks of the boar for a minute or so now, the rain making it harder to hear the footsteps. The sun is still not up either, making it hard to see the prey they stalk. Arella moves herself into a position where she can watch comfortably. She hauls herself up into an old oak tree. From her higher vantage point she can see the boar in the bushes. Arella's eyes see better in the dark, and she knows that she can see more here than Nashoba and Nootau.

Arella has to stifle a laugh as she watches the comedy show below her. As Nashoba and Nootau try to corner the boar, it simply runs in the opposite direction. Nootau dives for the boar in the dark but misses, landing in a muddy puddle. "This is ridiculous!" He shouts from the floor, slamming his fists into the ground. "We are never going to catch this…" Just as he is about to finish, he hears a terrifying squeal. Arella was too busy watching Nootau on the ground that she did not see Nashoba catch the boar with his dagger. The boar is now fuming, hot thick blood coming from the wound on its left shoulder. It turns on Nootau, still on the ground and charges at him. There is nothing Arella can do from up here. The branches are too close for her to take out her bow, and dropping to the ground from this height on the mud might cause her to slip, making her a target for the boar too.

Luckily, Nashoba knows that he is doing. He takes his dagger once again and lunges at the boar, landing on top of it. Covered in mud but determined, Nashoba drives the dagger into the neck of the boar, killing it outright. "You cut that one a bit fine didn't you?"

Nootau laughs from a foot away. "That thing nearly got me." They both start laughing, triumphant in their kill.

Over their heads, crows are flying, squawking as they go, all going in one direction. Arella looks up to the sky. It is turning orange. Nashoba and Nootau also look up at the sky with puzzled faces. As the sounds of the fleeing crows begins to die down, dread fills Arella's stomach. "The sun does not rise in that direction." Her fears are made worse. Smoke rises from the orange in the sky and screams are carried on the wind, coming from the direction of the village.

Chapter 3

Arella has a sinking feeling she knows what is happening at the village. She knows she has to do something, but it will get her seen. She cannot allow the village to be raided without her doing something about it. Arella has too much pride to let someone else fall because she is scared of being seen. Before she has chance to change her mind, Arella acts. She cups her hands to her mouth and howls, calling out for Maska in the way she said she would if she needed him. With his feline hearing, Maska will hear this, no matter where in the forest he is.

Nashoba and Nootau hear this noise and look up to the tree where Arella is hiding. They catch sight of her and are shocked, to stunned to speak. "White ghost." Nashoba blurts out. Arella glances down at them then leaps down out of the tree, landing perfectly on the slippy ground below. Her feet do not falter at all, and Arella is a little shocked by this. She takes flight and starts running towards Nashoba and Nootau. Nashoba takes his dagger in hand and aims if at Arella, thinking she is running for him. Arella runs straight past him, almost like he is not even there. He and Nashoba stare at her as she runs, struggling to work out what is going on, and if they really saw her again, The White Ghost.

With confident steps, Arella makes her way through the forest, towards the sounds of chaos and away from sanity. Thoughts flit through her mind as she runs. "What am I doing? This is madness. I'm going to get myself killed." But it doesn't matter. She cannot let the raid go ahead, and she must do something to stop it, or at least stop too many people getting hurt. She has heard many stories of raids on villages, and many people dying. This thought pushes her on faster.

Nashoba and Nootau look at each other. "What was all that about?" Then they hear it too, the sounds of screams filling the empty air. They too then take flight, running in the direction of the smoke, the fire and the screams.

Feeling the urgency to get there, and possibly the dangers of what might come when she enters the edge of the forest where the village is, Arella calls out once again to Maska, cupping her hands to her mouth and howling. As the sounds grow louder, so too does her dread. She does not know what she will find when she reaches the village, but it can't be anything good.

Hearing footsteps behind her pushes Arella on faster. She knew Nashoba and Nootau would not be far behind once they realised what was going on, and the footsteps confirm this. As she comes closer to the village, the screams become deafeningly loud, and the sound of fire crackling can be heard. Arella can also hear the gruff shouts of men, and the neigh of horses.

As she steps out from the treeline, closely followed by Nashoba and Nootau, Arella draws her bow, knocks and arrow, takes aim and fires. Her arrow finds the spot between the shoulder blades of a tall man dressed in dark boar skins. He shouts out in pain, turning to find the one who shot him. His eyes lock directly on Arella, her hood blown back by the wind, revealing the silvery white hair and pale skin beneath. "You little bitch!" He shouts at Arella through gritted yellow teeth. "I'm going to cut you open and gut you like a boar." He starts walking towards her, a large bloody dagger in his hand, the body of a young boy on the floor behind him, bleeding but alive. Arella knocks another arrow and fires, this time the arrow finding the left breast of the invader, piercing the tough hide of his clothes and lodging its self in his heart. With clumsy hands, the invader grasps at the arrow, falling to his knees. He looks at her again, the light leaving his eyes as he falls to the floor.

Arella looks up from the bleeding body on the floor before her, takes up her bow and aims again. This time a harder target. A man stands in the centre of the village, the muscles in his arms bigger than a bear, his skin as dark as one too. In his hand is a terrifying weapon, made from hard stone, a club of sorts. He swings the club back and forth, catching people with it as they attempt to defend themselves, causing each one to fly backwards, killing one man outright by crushing his skull. He laughs as blood splatters his weapon and his face. Arella takes aim on him, shooting for his hand, forcing him to drop the club. The arrow hits its mark, causing the beast to cry out in pain, Arella's arrow sticking out of his hand. He scowls, hate in his eyes and charges for her. The ground shakes with each step he takes. Arella reaches for an arrow from her quiver but her hands are not fast enough. The beast catches her in the stomach and drives her to the ground.

With the wind knocked out of her, Arella is only aware that the pressure from the beast's great bulk is no longer there. She braces herself for the inevitable thud that will come, the pain and the end of her life, but it does not come. Instead she hears a load roar coming from behind her. The black shape them jumps straight over her, landing square on the chest of the beast, knocking him backwards. Arella recovers her footing in time to see Maska tearing at the throat of the beast. He dies with gurgles as the blood escapes his body through the gaping wound in his neck.

"Glad you could join me Maska." Arella says to the great auron cat. His eyes look behind her and Arella turns to follow his gaze. She sees Nashoba and Nootau standing, staring, not moving, mouths open in shock. "Are you going to help or just stand there catching flies?" Arella says to them, amused by her own whit. Arella is drawn back into the raid by the sound of a woman screaming. She looks at Maska who instantly runs towards the noise. Arella half recognises the voice, but from Nashoba's reaction, he knows exactly who it is. He charges past Arella, following Maska to the sound of the screaming.

As Arella rounds the corner, past the centre tent, a man's screams join the woman. Arella sees Maska dragging the man away from the woman, teeth dug deep into his shoulder. The man swats at Maska, but is unable to get free. Arella glances at the woman crying on the floor, sobs rocking her thin frame. She is leaning over a man laid on the ground, a heavy wound to his stomach. "Please don't die Chogan. I need you to keep breathing." Nova sobs. Her brother holding her shoulder for comfort. Arella rounds on the murderer Maska has pinned. She aims her bow, watched by the others that gather at the scene. She pulls back the arrow tight, and with shaking hands, fires the arrow directly at the man's head. The arrow strikes his right eye, going deep into his brain and killing him outright.

Maska drops the body then turns to look for another victim. Arella can tell he is enjoying himself. Maska always loves to hunt, although humans might be taking things too far. He would do anything Arella would ask him to do. She looks at him. She thinks again. "Only the ones in the boar skin clothes Maska, and be careful." He nods his head and runs off in search of prey. Arella surveys her surroundings. Tents on fire, the rain keeping the fires low but not stopping the ones already lit from burning, blood on the floor at her feet, churned up with the mud. All around her, Arella can see bodies and people hurt, both villagers and invaders. Behind Arella, Nova cradles Chogan's lifeless body, crying out for him to not be dead, her dries falling on deaf ears.

On the other side of the village, Arella spots Mato and Doahte. They are fighting with a man on horseback, struggling to get a decent swing on him with their daggers. Arella moves closer to them, keeping one eye on the fights going on around her. Once she is within striking distance, she takes aim and launches her dagger at the man, hitting his square in the chest, causing him to fall from his mount. The horse gallops off a little way, then stops by the cow pen. Arella continues over to the man with her dagger lodged in his chest, takes hold of the red hilt and pulls it free. She wipes her dagger clean on her cloak, then sheaths it in her boot again.

A new confidence has come over Arella. This is the first time she has had proper practice of fighting since that day with Wolf, Goat, Bison and Fox, and she is actually very good at it. As she turns to walk away from Mato and Doahte, she bows slightly, a smile creeping onto her face as she leaves. They just stare at each other, stunned. Arella then moves onto another target, a young man chasing after a small child, attempting to cut her with a dagger. Arella moves quickly, careful not to slip on the muddy ground. She comes up close to the skinny man, directing her dagger at his back but not letting it pierce his skin. "Since when was chasing little girls around with a dagger fair?" She asks him.

"Killing little girls is easy. Their flesh is soft and they scream delightfully." He sniggers, not sign of fear in his voice. Arella looks down at the little girl, cowering on the floor, tears streaming down her face. She couldn't be any older than about five. Arella then searches the crowds for the little girl's mother and finds her, or what she thinks is her, struggling with an attacker of her own. Before Arella can open her mouth to call Maska for her, he is already there, dealing with the threat. The mother quickly runs over to the little girl, scooping her up into her arms, mouthing "thank you" as she goes.

"How would you like it if the tables were turned? If a little girl killed you?" the skinny man pauses, not sure what to say. Arella drives the dagger into his back, up into his heart through his ribs. She lets him drop to the ground, his blood pooling on the floor.

Arella surveys the carnage around her. Maska looks up at her, asking her for permission to go off and kill on his own. Arella knows that Maska likes hunting, but maybe humans is going a step too far. There isn't much of a choice though. Arella either lets Maska continue to kill the invaders, or more villagers die. "Only the ones in boar skins, and be careful." She says to him, giving him her blessing to take out the invaders. She turns to see if anyone else needs her help. Nashoba is distracted by his sister and her intended husband on the floor, Nootau has run to join the fight.

Turning to look at the battle again, Arella can see it is almost over. There are not many invaders left now in the village, and those that are still alive won't be for long. She takes another look and sees the devastation the invasion has left in its wake. There are bodies of men, women and worst of all children lying broken and bleeding on the floor, cries of pain from those still not dead, and those beginning to mourn their lost loved ones.

Commotion on the other side of the village draws Arella's attention. It is Maska. Some of the remaining warrior villages from this village have spotted him and are attempting to catch him. They must think he is here to take the bodies of the dead, to feed on their loved ones, but Arella knows that is not the case. She knows he is there to help, just like her. She strides over to Maska and the warriors with purpose. "Leave him alone." She says forcefully. She raises her bow, an arrow already aimed at one of the men attempting to capture Maska. She doesn't want to shoot one of the people she was attempting to help, but she would do it to save Maska. "He's done nothing wrong and he's here with me." She states. Just as she is about to continue, Arella feels pressure on her back and is thrown forwards. "It's your fault he's dead!" Nova screams at her. "You killed him, you brought the bad luck here, you lead the invaders here!" Arella does not understand. She was here to help, she arrived after the invaders. How can Nashoba's little sister think it was her fault this happened.

"It wasn't me." Arella pleads. "I didn't bring anyone here. I came to help when i saw the fire and heard the screams." She tries to convince Nova she is telling the truth, but the dark skinned girl is having none of it.

"It's your fault!" She yells again. Nashoba pulls his sister back.

"I think you'd better go." He says, not even looking Arella in the eye. This hurts, but Arella must keep herself strong. She looks towards Maska, pulls herself up from the ground and starts to walk away, through the village, past the bodies, followed by her great black auron cat, back into the forest and back into loneliness. As she goes, Arella hears an argument break out. She does not turn to see who is arguing, she doesn't want to.

Chapter 4

Back at her home in the forest, wrapped only in a clean set of furs, the rest of her clothes clean but wet, hung to dry over the fire, Arella sits. Maska has huddled up close to her to keep her warm, but it is not the air making her cold. She genuinely thought that if she helped the village, that they might not push her away, they might not make her feel so unwanted, but she was wrong. She put her life at risk, and that of Maska's for nothing. For all she knows that invasion might have ended no different if she were not there. Arella's sadness is taken over by anger. "How dare she say that to me." Arella suddenly blurts out, causing Maska to jump. "All I did was help them. Is it my fault her boyfriend couldn't defend himself." Arella feels bad as soon as she's said this. She knows that losing someone is hard, but she is sick of being blamed for things that are not her fault. She looks up at the sky, the clouds now breaking to reveal the blue sky above her.

While Arella sits back at the treehouse, clearly upset by what happened in the village, Maska decides the best thing he can do is go off into the forest and leave Arella to sort herself out. Nothing he could do now would cheer her up right now.

As he ventures further into the forest, further away from the treehouse, Maska starts to pick up the trail of the motto dear. He smells the air, the sweet musty smell of motto dear in rut fills his nostrils. He breaths deep, pinpointing the direction the smell is coming from. His eyes dart to the left. That way. With careful steps, Maska walks towards the smell, allowing it to fill his lungs and lead him towards his prey. He glances down at the ground, checking his footing. Maska spots the motto deer's cloven hoof prints in the fresh mud. He follows them as well as the smell. From the amount of prints on the ground, the herd will be about thirty strong, plenty of prey for him to choose from.

Staying low as he moves through the undergrowth, Maska hears them before he sees them. Tiny horns clashing with one another, fighting for position as head buck. Maska peers through the bushes, watching the deer for a few minutes. He is looking for a young deer, their meat is the most tender, but he does not want one that looks sickly, nor does he want to have to work too hard for his meal. After watching them graze and butt heads for a couple of minutes, Maska spots the deer he would like to take home for Arella. It looks to be a young male, tiny horns beginning to grow on its head, possibly one of the young from last year. It is not too old to be tough meat, but old enough that it has no more growing to do.

Readying himself for pouncing, Maska gets himself low to the ground. He steps forwards, careful not to crunch the dead leaves with his big paws. He crawls across the ground, as close to the deer as he can get while still being in the cover of the bushes. One of the sentry deer calls out a warning. It has caught Maska's scent on the wind. He knew he forgot to check something. When Arella is with his, she always remembers this.

The deer take off, running as quick as their little legs can carry them in the opposite direction to Maska. He gets up from his crouched position quickly, catching up to the deer without must trouble. They duck adn weave through the tight undergrowth, followed close by Maska. The young deer he had his mind set on is trailing close to the back, a slow start after the others. Maska catches the back legs of the deer as it runs, pulling it off balance. The young buck tumbles to the floor, Maska on top of him before he can get his footing again. With one swift bite to the jugular, the motto dear is dead, and Maska has food to take back to Arella for when she wakes up. He lifts his head, proud of his achievement.

The motto deer is heavy, but Maska is strong enough to carry it back to the treehouse without too much hassle. Careful not to drag the deer through the mud on the ground, Maska brings his prize back to Arella. As he steps into the clearing, he finds her already awake. Her hair is wet and she looks refreshed. "Thought you'd be back soon." Arella smiles. She always looks better when she has slept well. "I see motto deer. Aww Maska, you got that for me?" She smiles again, bigger this time. "Well, thank you." She walks over to him, takes the deer from his jaws and takes it to the ground hut. Arella then hooks the barb of an anamoa branch through the neck of the deer and hangs it from one of the high branches. In the quickly cooling autumn air, the meat will keep fresh for a good few days.

"So what are we doing today then Maska?" Arella asks. He just blinks at her. "Well we can't just sit around here all day." Maska disagrees. He's done his running around for the day, and would quite happily sit around and laze in the remaining autumn sun. It is late in the day anyway, and the sun is high in the sky. "Well I want to go out even if you don't." She smiles. I'm going for a run then Maska, I need to burn some energy off." She pulls her cloak off, lettitting it fall behind her, pulling her hair out from underneath her top, then ties it up in a loose ponytail behind her head then begins her stretches.

Careful not to miss any of her muscles when she stretches, Arella relays information to Maska. "So I shouldn't be gone long, but you never know. I aim to be back before midnight." Maska looks at her. "What? I feel like I need a long run." She continues stretching. "Anyway, you'll be okay on your own here, and you have food in the treehouse. Just follow my tracks if you need me Maska." She walks over to the great auron cat and ruffles the long fur on the top of his head, the purple flecks shimmer in the sunlight. He purrs at her touch. "Promise I won't be long." She says to him as she leaves.

Through the trees Arella runs, dodging the roots that tangle on the floor, ducking under low hanging trees and vines that threaten to catch her hair. She truly feels free now, running in the wild like this. This is when Arella feels most at home, able to do what she wants to do. The dream she had years ago has come true. She is living on her own, with no one to tell her what to do, and nothing to stop her from being herself. Despite the tragedies from the night before, Arella is happy. Although thinking about this brings her some sadness. She might not have known Chogan, the young man who lost his life to the hoard of invaders, or Nova, Nashoba's little sister, racked with sadness at the loss of the man she loved, but it is still sad. Arella feels she must visit the village, to check what state they are in this afternoon, see if there is anything she might be able to do to help them. Not that they would want her help, but she has to at least make sure Nashoba is okay. Arella is not sure why she is so obsessed with Nashoba, maybe it is his green eyes, but she cannot stop thinking about him, hoping he is okay, wishing she could see him again.

Arella stops to catch her breath. Running fast is what Arella does best, but when she has been running a while, she gets tired. She stops to take in her surroundings, to work out which way would be best to go to get to the village. She decided that through the clearing might not be such a good idea. They know she has been there, and more than once. If the men from the village came looking for her, this is the first place they would come.

After deciding that going round towards the north side of the village would be best, so this is what she does. Backtracking on herself a little as she goes, Arella jogs through the trees towards the village, dropping her pace so she can listen out for the sounds of people moving. She does not want to be spotted now. Not when the villagers are so angry and upset, and most likely on guard.

The trees in this part of the forest are closer together, harder to make your way through quickly. Arella slows to a walk, calming her breathing as she does this. She is close to the village now, and must be careful. No doubt someone will be on guard close by, making sure no other invaders hit while they are down. As Arella reaches the edge of the bank of trees lining the north side of the village, shivers come over her. Most of the tents are broken, smouldering or torn. Crying can be heard close to Arella. She moves her gaze towards the noise, finding a large group of people gathered around. In the middle of the group, Arella can see something, but she is not sure what it is.

In the crowd, Arella spots faces she recognises. The first person she sees is Nashoba, his green eyes wet with tears, his younger sister's face buried into his chest, shaking as she cries. Arella cannot see her face, covered by long black hair, but everything about the way she moves tell Arella what is in the middle of the group of people. When Arella left the village the day before, Chogan had been alive, barely breathing but still alive. In between the quiet sobs of those around the lifeless body of Chogan, Arella can her bits of whispered conversations. "Why would they attack our village? We have nothing of value."

"How did they know where we were?"

"How many of them were there, it seemed like a lot?"

"Did we lost many people, or was it just Chogan?"

"So young, too young to die."

"He didn't even know how to fight properly yet."

"Such potential, sure a lovely boy."

"Did you see that white girl?"

"Yeah her and that demon cat."

This is broken when Nashoba makes his announcement. "We must take the body of Chogan and the others we've lost to the black stone in the middle of the meadow, bury them there." Nashoba says, the tears from his eyes never escaping, but still moisture threatens to fall. His sister lifts her head, eyes red and puffy, her face wet with tears.

"He always loved the meadow. It's where he'd want to be buried." Her voice breaks but she continues to talk. "Ujarak, would you do the ceremony?" She asks the old man. From the other side of the group, with his back to Arella, the old man bows his head.

"I would be honoured Nova."

Arella follows the group of men and women into the meadow, following around the side, careful to stick to the trees where she wouldn't be seen. Not that anyone is in the right frame of mind to be looking out for her. Arella is suddenly aware that she is not wearing her cloak. She is totally exposed to the eyes of the villagers, if there were to look her way. Her white hair would give her away easy if they were to look. Luckily, the sun is bright today, and they are too upset to watch. Arella thinks for a second, then thrusts her hands into the mud on the ground. She pauses before smothering the mud all over her face, arms and in her hair helping to camouflage herself a little. This way she can watch without anyone knowing where she is. The mud id starting to dry and crack on her skin. It feels strange, but it's the only way she feels safe watching, knowing she won't be seen by the other villagers

This feels a little wrong, hiding in the treeline to watch a funeral, but Arella is intrigued. She has never seen a funeral before, unable to watch in her old village, and she has no idea what happens.

From the edge of the meadow, hidden by long grasses, Arella watches the funeral of the man she didn't know. She watches as the strong men, Nashoba, Nootau and Mato included carry Chogan's lifeless body on a wooden board to the black stone close to the edge of the meadow. Joining the others already in the meadow, Arella notices that most of the bodies are adults, but a couple of children are also there. Their bodies covered in bright patttterns. Their funerals have already finished. A few men are digging graves in the meadow while the ceremony takes place. They set it down carefully. Ujarak moves forwards towards Chogan's body. With a full headdress of brightly coloured feathers, Ujarak paints patterns on Chogan's body. It is only now that Arella realises he is not wearing anything on his chest. The wound caused by the invader has been sewn up, and the blood gone from his bare skin, looking cold and a little paler than before. The patterns Ujarak paints on Chogan's body are in white. "The circles I paint represent everlasting life, so Chogan may leave his body and his spirit may live on within us all." He then moves on to draw white circles on what Arella can only assume to be close members of his family and friends. One older woman seems to be crying uncontrollably. This must be his mother. She is a pretty woman, hair slightly greying, but youth still in her eyes.

Ujarak then moves back Chogan's body. He starts painting swirls and spirals onto his cold skin. "These symbols represent the life that Chogan had, and how it had a beginning and an end." He then moves to paint on others again. When he gets to Nova, she lets a tear fall. Nashoba puts his arm around her, making her look small. Another tear falls at his touch, but she does not break. She is trying to be strong, but someone so young should not have to see their loved one die.

Finally, small dots are painted onto Chogan's skin. "This represents the stars in the sky, and the spirits that will guide Chogan to the spirit realm, where he will watch over us all, and especially over you Nova." Ujarak says. With this, Nova cannot hold her tears in anymore. She makes no noise, but let's hot tears fall freely from her eyes. As Arella watches, a small tear escapes her. She does not even realise she is crying. Such a sad moment, but very touching and lovely to watch. Arella wonders if her mother got a funeral like this when she died, but she doubts it.

Once the body painting has been completed, and a fire built on the black rocks, Nashoba and Mato begin digging Chogan's grave. A shallow hole, about four foot deep and six foot long is dug. The chanting begins, slow and quiet. Ujarak starts it off, slowly joined by other members of the tribe.

'We are the stars which sing,

We sing with our light;

We are the birds of fire,

We fly over the sky.

Our light is a voice;

We make a road for the spirits;

For the spirits to pass over.

Among us are three hunters

Who chase a bear.

There never was a time

When they were not hunting.

We look down on the mountains

This is the song of the stars.'

Arella feels heat on her cheeks and realises she's crying again. She wipes the tears from her face and decides she should leave the grieving tribe to it. She got what she came for. She now knows that no one else in the tribe died, and that Nashoba is alive.

Arella looks behind her, checking there is no one to step into. When she turns, she comes face to face with the little girl she saved yesterday. The girl is startled to see Arella and falls backwards. She is about to scream but Arella stops her. She moves forwards, cupping her hand to the little girl's mouth. "Please don't scream." She pleads at the girl, careful to keep her voice low. The girls eyes change, she recognises Arella's purple eyes. She sees this and taking a chance, removes her hand from the girl's face. "You remember me from yesterday?" Arella asks. The little girl nods her small head, dark hair bobbing around as she does so.

"Thank you." She whispers.

"Were you watching too?" Arella asks. The little girl nods at her. "We're you not allowed to go and watch?"

"Children aren't allowed to go to funerals. I wanted to, Chogan was nice to me, but I wasn't allowed." The little girl starts to sob. Arella reaches out for her, taking her into her arms.

"Don't cry. Funerals are sad. You wouldn't have wanted to be there anyway. You can say goodbye to Chogan from here though." Arella tries to comfort the little girl.

"What's your name?" The little girl asks, her mud brown eyes still wet with tears, shaking in her voice.

"Arella." She answers.

"I'm Ayasha." She says, smiling. "You look funny." A little giggle escapes her mouth.

"Thank you Ayasha. But I think you look funny." Arella ruffles the girls messy hair. "You can't tell anyone you saw me though." Arella whispers.

"Why not? Everyone saw you yesterday."

"Not everyone is very happy with me coming here yesterday, and I really don't want to upset anyone." Arella answers. Ayasha seems to understand this.

"You can be our little secret." She whispers, putting her forefinger to her mouth and saying "Shhhh." Arella laughs quietly at this.

"I have to go now Ayasha, but I will be back at some point. I can promise you that." Arella says to her. She then takes one last look behind her, at the funeral for the boy she did not know and she moves away, back towards the forest.

As she leaves the meadow, Arella hears Nashoba's voice loud and clear. "Tonight, we don't mourn the death of Chogan, we celebrate his life and everything he brought to us." This makes Arella smile. It's nice to know that tonight will not just be sadness. The sun is on its way down now, and the sky is a beautiful bright pink, flecked with orange. A few clouds still hang around in the sky, but no threat of rain.

Once safely back in the cover of the trees, Arella starts running. This is what she really came out here for, and it is what she intends to do still. With another hour of daylight left still, Arella can get a decent run from her trip. She wasted a lot of time at the village, but she would not have settled if she did not know that they were okay.

With slippery mud underfoot, running is not so easy. Arella has to use more muscles, and more thinking than she would normally do on a run. By the time she gets back to the treehouse she is well and truly knackered. When she returns, she finds that Maska is not there, no doubt out chasing rabbits or prowling the perimeter of his territory. Arella takes straight to the water, to wash away her camouflage and clean off her clothes.

The water is cold when she steps into it, but Arella like this. The dry mud on her skin was starting to itch. It feels nice to be free of it again. She quickly washes herself, cleans her clothes then gets out. She puts clean clothes on and her boots before leaving the water's edge to hang her clothes to dry. She hangs them in the ground hut where her and Maska usually eat and rest during the day. With the autumn air getting colder, Arella feels the need to put her cloak on. It takes the chill off, but she can still feel the bite of the wind. A fire is needed to take that away. Arella sets to work on building a fire, and in no time at all, it has roared into life and lights up the clearing. Stars have started to peek through the blackness above, but with no moon in the sky tonight, it is darker than normal.

Arella tends to the chickens, while it is still light enough to do so. She makes sure they have food, and checks the nests for eggs. It has been a couple of days since she did this, so she is expecting there to be a couple at least. Arella will not let the chickens sit on any eggs now. Chicks born this late in the year would probably not survive the cold winter. She will instead eat any eggs that are laid.

Adding the six eggs she found in the nests to the seven she got from the other day, Arella smiles. Eggs last about a month after they have been laid, and with the amount she is getting, she will be able to eat them through most of winter. Her chickens will stop laying when the snow starts to fall, but it should only fall for a couple of weeks.

"I should get some food ready for when Maska comes home." Arella says to herself. She proceeds to prepare the motto deer he caught just the day before, skinning, gutting and portioning the meat. Some of it can be kept for another couple of days before cooking, but Arella will cook about half of the carcass tonight. The cooked meat will then last another couple of days, and they will be set for food for the rest of the week. Or at least Arella will. Maska eats a lot more than she does. She wouldn't be surprised if Maska was out hunting for rabbits right now. Arella laughs. Maska always looks runny when he's hunting. He stays low to the ground, but he always wiggles his bum before he pounces.

The smell of cooking food must have reached Maska, because not long after Arella places a motto deer leg over the open flames, he arrives through the bushes, dirty and covered in leaves. "Stop right there!" Arella says to him. "There is no way on this planet you are coming anywhere near the treehouse looking like that." Maska tilts his head to the side and blinks, his odd coloured eyes sparkle with mischief. "Get in that lake and wash yourself off before you come into the hut." Arella teases. Maska steps towards her, intent filling his feline features. He comes close to Arella, but does not touch her. He knows that if he got her muddy when she has clearly just washed, he would be in big trouble. He heads for the lake to clean himself up while Arella continues to cook the motto deer, his tummy rumbling audibly. "You shouldn't even be hungry, with all the rabbits you ate yesterday." Arella laughs.

Chapter five

After a good meal and a long sleep, Arella wakes up feeling refreshed. When she opens her eyes, Arella can see the fog that covers the forest in the mornings. It will burn off soon, but always makes her home look more mysterious. She stretches her arms and legs, her back clicking as she sits up. "I slept really well last night Maska." She says. The great auron cat beside her grumbles his response. I'm guessing you're not ready to get up yet then?" She says to him. He looks at her through half open eyes, only a sliver of green and yellow visible. Arella laughs. "Okay well I'm going to make breakfast. You come join me when you're awake.

Arella leaves the treehouse, taking her boots and cloak on her way down the tree. She jumps from half way down the tree, landing on the drying ground with a thud. The chickens start to cluck as she hits the floor. She must have woken them. This brings more grumbles from Maska. "They'll quieten down soon Maska, don't worry yourself." She laughs again. He is funny when he's in a bad mood, which is every morning. The auron cat is not a morning person at all.

Arella takes three of the eggs from the ground hut, cracks and places them on a flat black rock, then starts a fire. Once the fire is going, Arella places the black rock over the flames to cook. "Nothing better than fresh eggs." Arella says to herself. "Enough to set me up for the day." She gathers some berries from one of the nearby bushes and munches on them while she waits for the eggs to cook. Maska soon joins her, the fur on the left hand side of his head stuck down, and the fur on the right spiked up. Arella nearly chokes on a berry at the sight of him. "Come here silly cat." She says to him as she flattens his fur back down, making him look more presentable. Maska purrs at her touch. He sits next to her on the dry mossy ground, cleaning his paws and face while Arella eats her eggs.

"So what are we doing today Maska?" Arella asks the cat, her mouth full of eggs. He just blinks at her as if to say, "Whatever you want to do."

"I just don't know though." She pauses while she finished her eggs. "I tell you what I would like to do. I'd like to run with the wolves." She looks at Maska expectantly. "Do you think they would let me run with them, watch them hunt? I think it's fascinating watching a pack hunt." Maska turns away from her. "Not that I don't like watching you hunt too, but I would like to see how a pack of wolves can take down something as big as a buffalo. You never know, it might even give us some tips of how to take out bigger prey." Maska seems to soften at this. "You don't have to come with me if you don't want to though Maska. You can hang around here, patrol your territory, anything you want to do." Maska seems to like this idea.

Maska climbs back up into the treehouse, clearly wanting to go back to bed for a bit, but Arella is wide awake. "Well you can come find me if you need me." She says to him. He chuffs at her, lettiting her know he understands, then disappears from sight into the vine covered house. Arella swaps her doe skinned cloak for her fur one. This she made recently, after finding out that winters got pretty cold in the forest when there wasn't a fire burning constantly. Especially when Maska leaves to go for a night time walk, or when he was out hunting without her. She made it from a mix of rabbit and paloa fox fur, all sewn together, the fur on the outside. It is very warm in this cloak, but just what Arella needs today. The wind has picked up, and it is rather cold. She pulls the hood up around her face, leaving her hair down today to help with the cold also, then starts walking away from her home, making sure her dagger is in her boot, and picking up her grathon on her way, leaving Maska and walking into the forest and in the direction of her old village.

Arella comes to the edge of the forest, the plains in front of her sparkling with the morning frost. The village she used to live in is no longer there, raided by an invading tribe just last year. The few remaining villagers left the site, feeling that it was damned by evil spirits for all the bad things that kept happening to them. Remnants of the village still remain, although nature has taken most of it back over again. As Arella walks towards the stream that used to run by the side of the village, the last place she saw the pack of wolves that live in this area, she feels a chill run down her spine. It feels as though someone is watching her. She turns quickly, looking towards the bushes behind her, but cannot see anything. She shrugs her shoulders. "Probably just a fox." She says to herself, and carries on walking.

  The bushes that line the banks of the stream have grown bigger in the four years that Arella has been away from the village. She prefers the way it looks now though, not tainted by humans and their pollution. She moves closer to the water where she searches for tracks to follow. She finds one, a singular paw print. "Yes." She celebrates. She looks around the bank of the stream for more and soon finds them. The wolves were here, and more recently than a couple of days ago, these tracks are fresh. She follows them over to the other side of the stream and through the large rocks. The tracks are faint on the ground here. It is dry, and the prints are hard to see. There are small indentations in the ground, but if Arella was paying less attention, she could easily go off track.

A crack of a branch behind her makes Arella jump. She turns quickly but there is nothing there. She decides to ignore it. Whatever made that noise does not sound big enough to harm her, and with the wolves so close, it would be stupid to try. A howl from a wolf close by makes Arella Jump. She is on edge now, but probably a good thing. She turns back round to find a large grey wolf staring at her, his yellow eyes focused on her purple ones. She stops moving, lowers her grathon, which she raised upon hearing the howl, and bows a little, always keeping eyes focused on the wolf. She does not look the wolf directly in the eyes. This would be seen as challenging him, instead she looks at his ears, watching them for changes in his mood. They are up at the moment, on high alert. Arella knows these wolves well. She sees them in the forest a lot, but never has she gotten this close to them without Maska. She has no doubt that they will not attack her, and that if one of them did, she would be able to fend them off. This pack is small, consisting of only six wolves, and they are all smaller than average.

The wolf considers Arella for a couple of minutes, walking around her, sniffing at the air, judging what to think of her. After a couple of minutes of this, Arella's heart beating fast all the while, the wolf turns away from her and walks away. She watches him go, then slowly follows. The wolf turns to look at her when he hears her footsteps, but does not stop or make a move on her. He is inviting her into the pack.

As Arella approaches the other wolves, they regard her with caution. The beta wolf that led Arella into the pack leads her directly to the alpha. He is sat atop a large flat rock, his mate sitting next to him, her belly swollen with pups. He growls low at Arella, his thick black coat shaking with the rumble. Arella lowers her head in respect, and the alpha backs down. He looks her up and down, before leaving his post on the rock to investigate her. It does not take him long to do this, and after less than a minute, he walks away from her and returns to his rock. He has accepted her, and Arella is now able to be with the wolves without fear that she will be attacked or rejected.

One of the smaller wolves, a slight deep brown female walks over to Arella, her head held low, tail between her legs. Arella lowers herself to the ground, coming down to the same level as the beta female. The female sniffs at Arella's boots, smelling the mud and leaves that she has walked through. Arella extends her hand to the female. She backs off quickly, then looks at Arella's hand. She does not move, staying perfectly still, waiting for the wolf to make her move. Eventually the beta wolf moves to the hand, sniffing it. She moves even closer and licks Arella's hand, Arella relaxes a little more, letting the beta wolf get closer to her. The small female moves closer to Arella and licks her face. From watching this pack over the previous years, Arella has noticed a lot about their behaviour. She knows the pecking order, and who is alpha, but she also knows the different submission and dominance signs. Face licking is one of the things beta wolves do to gain the approval of a higher member of the pack. This beta clearly regards Arella as a higher member, as she was accepted directly by the alpha. This is a good thing though, it means that she has the acceptance of the whole pack. They will now let her run with them. This is exactly what she wanted from the pack.

Slowly the other beta wolves descend on Arella, each of them accepting her in their own way. Arella wasn't quite sure this would ever work. It was a huge risk to take herself into the middle of a wolf pack and expect them to take to her, but her bet paid off.

After lazing around with the wolves for a good half hour, the Alpha gets up from his post, deciding it is time to go hunting. With his mate heavily pregnant, he does not have a full pack to hunt with. His decision is to leave her behind, and also the young brown female beta that first accepted Arella. The alpha looks at Arella. She doesn't know what he wants her to do. He then looks from her to the bloodglass grathon on the ground next to her. Arella speaks out quietly, not wanting to frighten the alpha. "I can hunt with you." She says. The lowers his head, then looks at her through bright yellow eyes. She takes this as an invitation to hunt.

The pack has picked up the scent of a herd of buffalo. The alpha picks up pace, and the other three wolves shadow him, closely followed by Arella. The wolves do not travel far before finding the herd. They can't have been running for more than five minutes. Arella hears the buffalo before she sees them. It is a large herd, and the smell if overpowering. They come to the top of a hill, and spot the buffalo at the bottom, dozens of them all gathers close to a small lake. There are no young with them at this time of year, but a few older weaker looking animals.

The alpha takes the lead down the hill towards his prey, seeking out the one he would like to take the kill home. He moves to the left of the herd. They have not yet spotted the pack coming, but that will soon be changed. A gust of wind comes from behind the pack, heading straight in the direction of the bathing buffalo. They catch scent of this and immediately start running in the opposite direction.

The alpha moves to the left, and so do the others. Arella follows suit, following one of the beta wolves and taking direction from the alpha. Once they reach the bottom of the hill and the back of the herd, the pack split in two. The alpha and one of the beta's going one way, while the other two beta's veer off to the right. Arella follows the two beta's to the right, keeping close to them as she can. She watches the alpha through the legs of the running buffalo, their panicked cries and thumping hooves deafening in her ears. Clouds of dust rise into the air as the many hoofs and paws hit the ground, the pack running alongside the herd for a minute or so, snapping at ankles as they go.

The alpha is focused on his target ahead. Arella follows his gaze and spots his mark. One of the buffalo in the herd is limping on her front leg. The other wolves have now also marked this buffalo as their target and close in on him

The red stone wolf around Arella's neck bounces as she runs, using all her speed to keep up with the pack and the buffalo. As the alpha hones in on his target, and the others follow suit. As the pack close in on the buffalo, now separated from the rest of the herd, Arella stands back a little out of the way. It thrashes its horned head around in an attempt to deter the wolves, narrowly missing one of the darker females. She ducks out of the way then dives for the buffalo's neck, misses and backs of quickly.

For an animal with a limp, the buffalo is certainly fighting hard. Arella takes her grathon in hand and just as she is about to lunge for the buffalo, something catches her from behind. She flies into the air, searing pain in her back before hitting the hard red ground beneath her. Even with the rains softening it underneath, the surface is hard and stony. Arella places her hand on the spot on her back with the most pain. It's hot and wet. Blood. Arella feels hot and sick, her vision starts to blur. She never liked blood, and seeing her own is worse than seeing someone else's. She steadies herself to face her attacker and finds a strong male buffalo just a few meters away from her, his head held low, huffing steam from his nostrils, Arella's blood on one of his horns. It scrapes a giant hoof on the stony floor, readying its self for charging again.

Behind her, Arella can hear the struggles of the buffalo as it is taken down by the wolves. They are directly behind her, and the buffalo directly in front of her. She is in the middle, and that is why the buffalo is attacking her. It thinks she is standing in the way of it and the buffalo the wolves are taking down. She has to move quickly. If she does not, the buffalo will gore her with his horns, and she will not be able to stop him.

The buffalo scrapes his hooven foot on the floor again, steam coming from his nose, grunting and grinding his teeth. He charges again for Arella. She rolls to the side, the pain in her back making her cry out. The buffalo misses her, scraping the floor with his great horns instead of Arella's body. She rolls onto her front, trying to ignore the pain in her back. Before she can get to her knees, the buffalo is on her. She rolls again, narrowly missed by the bufffalo's horns. She moves quicker this time, knowing the buffalo will come for her again. She quickly gets to her knees, the pain in her back hot. She takes her grathon in hand and turns. Just at the bufffalo comes for her, she gets to her feet and holds her grathon in both hands, the shaft in the middle the only thing stopping the bufffalo from goring her. His horns lock with the shaft of the grathon, pushing Arella backwards. She locks her legs in place but the buffalo is strong. He pushes her backwards causing her to fall back. As she falls backwards, Arella lets go of the grathon with one hand. the weapon shifts, its blade pointing to the sky. The wind is knocked out of Arella as she falls to the ground, then again as the buffalo falls on her.

Chapter 6

Arella pushes the great body of the bison off her, his blood covering her as she moves him. When she is finally free, she pulls the grathon from the bison's head. It struck him in the left eye, his horns narrowly missing her chest as he came down. The only thing stopping her from dying was the grathon and sheer luck. Arella, covered in the blood of the dead bison, looks up to the sky. "Thank you." She says to the spirits that kept her alive. Silence surrounds her for a second as she takes in her surroundings. The other bison have left, getting as far away from the bloodbath as they could. The wolves are behind Arella, they themselves are covered in blood, the blood of the bison they took down. Arella steps away from the body of the bison in front of her, proud and upset at the same time. She is impressed that she managed to take the beast down on her own. It really is a brute. But in the same way, she can't help but wonder if there was a way of getting away without having to kill it.

One of the beta wolves stares at Arella, the smaller brown female and the pregnant female close behind her. They must have either heard or smelled the kill and decided to find their pack. She has been left on the outside of the pack to wait her turn at the caucus, and is looking hungrily at Arella's kill. However much she would love to give her kill to this beta, Arella knows that she would anger the alpha. She lowers herself down to a crouch and growls at the female. She feels bad for her, but the hierarchy of the pack must stay intact.

Turning back to the bison, Arella takes her dagger from her boot and begins cutting at the skin of her kill. She may not use the meat, but the skin will make a healthy addition to her home, and extra furs are always welcome in the winter, especially the furs of a beast as big as this one. Although they will need a good clean to rid them of the smell. The pain in Arella's back flares up again, but she must work through the pain. Plus, she does not trust the wolves enough to let her guard down with them.

By the time she has finished removing the skin, the wolves have finished eating their bison. It was skinny, so the wolves are still hungry, and they have two mouths, and the soon to be pups to feed as well. The alpha stalks towards Arella, intent on taking her kill. She bows to him, picks up the furs and backs away from the caucus. The alpha is first with his head in the stomach of the bison, eating the nutritious insides of the bison. Arella turns away. She never liked watching Maska eat and although she got used to it, it is very different watching his eat a small rabbit or leg of a deer, than watching a pack of wolves tear through a bison's caucus.

Arella spots something on the top of the hill back towards where she first found the wolves. Her pulls her hand up to her eyes to shield them from the sun. The three figures move. Too small to be bears, but walking on two legs. People! But who is it? Arella hauls the skin onto her back and starts up the hill towards the figures. The move quickly when they notice she has spotted them.

Arella recognises the silhouettes, but cannot place them. There are not many people she knows so that narrows it down a bit. The pain in her back grows stronger as she reaches the summit of the hill. She places her hand on the wound, feeling the blood still seeping from it. She feels faint again. No matter how much she wants to find out who was watching her, she has to make sure this wound is not fatal first. She stops at the top of the hill, looking down on the other side. The figures are running now, looking over their shoulders as they go.

Arella drops the fur to the ground. She removes her cloak and lifts her shirt to reveal the wound. It stings as she removes the clothing from it, but the cool air on the gash is a blessing. Arella takes the bottom section of her shirt and rips it. She screws this into a ball then rips a section higher, this time all the way round. She holds the screwed up section of shirt to the wound, letting out a gasp of pain, then uses the rest of the torn shirt to tie it in place. She ties it as tight as her shaking hands can manage, the pain becoming too much for her to handle.

Tearing the shirt has left her midriff exposed, but it is better this than bleeding to death through the wound on her back. She pulls her cloak back on, drawing it as tight as she can, picks up the furs from the buffalo and her grathon and starts back down the hill towards the forest she calls home.

The walk home is hard, much harder than running with the wolves. Her fight with the bison has left Arella battered, bruised and bleeding. She drags her feet a little as she walks, every step painful and difficult. "Not how I intended today to end." She groans to herself as she comes up to the edge of the forest. The trees in front of her are darkening quickly, the sunlight fading. Arella has been out all day with the wolves, and it will be night soon. Ideally she would like to get back to the treehouse before nightfall. That way she will be able to clean and dress her wound in light, rather than dark. However, at the speed she is moving, she doubts she will manage it.

Arella stops about five minutes into the forest. Sickness comes over her and she retches as she leans against an old tree trunk. "Oh gods, I feel awful." She moans. She retches again but nothing comes up. It is only then that Arella realises she has not eaten since breakfast and there is probably nothing in her system. Her head begins to pound and she feels dizzy.

Sitting with her head between her knees, Arella breaths deep. After sitting for ten minutes, Arella starts to feel better. She still has a headache, but the dizzy and sickness feelings have gone away. She gets herself up from the ground slowly and continues walking.

Using the grathon for balance, Arella makes her way through the forest towards her home. It is only now that she hears it. Roaring. "Maska!" Arella gasps. She follows the sound of his voice as quickly as she can. His roaring grows louder and more desperate.

"Quickly before she gets here." A female voice says. Arella recognises it.

"Are you sure we should be doing this?" A man asks. Again she knows this voice. In her panic and debilitated state she cannot work out who it is. Maska roars out again.

"Shut that thing up before someone hears it." The woman says." Arella is getting closer, and the voices are growing louder. "It scratched me!" The woman shouts. "Nashoba kill it." Arella's heart drops. She now knows who it was watching her, and who is attaching Maska. Nova. She looked like a sweet innocent girl. Fuelled with rage, Arella pushes on faster.

"Should we be killing it at all?" Nashoba asks. Arella comes to the edge of the clearing where Maska is being attacked, again.

Arella drops her furs and grathon to the floor. The noise is notices and Nova turns to look at her. "Oh there she is. Just the person we came to see." Nova spits at Arella.

"Why are you here?" Arella asks, her eyes darting to Maska, a thick rope around his neck, tied to the very tree they call home, trying desperately to get free. "What did we ever do to you?"

"What did you to do me?" Nova laughs. "You killed my Chogan."

"What?" Arella is bemused. "I didn't kill him. And Maska definitely didn't. We weren't even there when he died." Nova laughs.

"You named that thing?" She laughs, looking at Maska then continues her rant. "It was you who caused his death though." Arella is confused. Her head hurts, her back hurts. She's tired, dehydrated and doesn't understand.

"How?"

"By being here." Nova says simply. "Ever since my brother saw you in the forest that day 'White Ghost', everything started going wrong. First my brother was taken away from me for four years…"

"That could not be helped Nova, you know that." Nashoba interrupts. Nova scowls at him.

"Then my father dies, now Chogan." She throws her arms in the air in anger. "If you'd have just stayed away we would all be just fine." Anger boils in Arella's blood.

"If it weren't for me, you brother and his friends would have all been killed by a rabid wolf!" Arella shouts. Maska roars in protest of being tied up. Nova lashes out, throwing a rock at him, hitting him on the top of the head. He cries out in pain, cowering against the tree they hold him captive at. Arella lunges forwards, screaming at Nova. She gets close to her, but before she can make contact she is caught. Big hands grab hold of her arms from behind her. Fingers dig into her upper arm, stopping her from moving. Arella looks behind her and finds the scarred face of Mato. "Let me go!" She shouts at her captor.

"If I let you go you'll kill Nova." He says calmly, as always the voice of reason. Arella's head starts to swim again, the loss of blood getting to her now. She's struggling to think straight and her vision is blurring. Arella shakes her head, trying to knock the creeping blackness away.

"So what if I do? She's hurting Maska." Arella's voice starts to break. Searing pain in her back causes her to cry out. Maska cries out when he hears her pain, trying desperately to get to her. Nova strikes him again, this time causing him to go unconscious. Arella screams out and thrashes her arms about. Mato can't hold his grip anymore and he lets her go, ripping the material on her sleeves as he does, scratching the delicate white skin underneath.

Arella lunges forwards for Nova, filled with rage and determination. She has never wanted to hurt someone as much as she wants to hurt Nova now. Not even with Wolf and her disciples all those years ago. It is not like her at all. Arella's anger pushes her through the pain and her hands find Nova's throat. The force at which she hits her sends them both flying to the ground. The wind is knocked out of Nova, preventing her from fighting back. The others around them stand around, shocked, unable to move or help Nova.

Arella keeps her hands pressed to Nova's throat until her face starts to change colour. A sudden realisation of what she is doing comes over her and she pulls her hands away, staring at them as if they don't belong to her. She gets up from her straddled position on top of Nova and crawls backwards. She looks over to Maska and rushes to his side, falling as she gets close to him. "Maska? Can you hear me? Oh please don't be dead." She starts to cry. She looks at the wound on his head. It is bleeding.

Behind her, Arella can hear the other men helping Nova to her feet. "That bitch just tried to kill me!" she gasps. "Did you see that?" She asks Nashoba.

"You did hit that auron cat of hers." He tries.

"Don't you dare defend her!" Nova shouts. "How dare you try to kill me!" She aims at Arella, but she is far too preoccupied to entertain her. Arella takes Maska's bleeding head in her hands, lifting it up onto her knees. The weight of his lifeless head crushing her fragile legs. The pain in her back has gone, but it now resonates through her chest. A tear falls from her cheek onto that of Maska's, wetting his black and purple fur. She looks down at his chest and her heart leaps. "He's still breathing." She says, a slight jolt of laughter escaping her. "Come on Maska, you can make it through." She says to the great cat. She rubs his shoulder, the fur soft but tangled. "Remind me when we get you better again that you need brushing." She says to him. At her touch and her voice, Maska's eyes flutter slightly.

"Can you even hear me?" Arella hears from behind her. "The stupid thing isn't even listening to me." Arella feels a sharp pain in her back as Nova's boot connects. She cries out.

"Nova stop. This is going too far." Mato says to her, but to no avail. Nova kicks Arella again, this time causing the wound on her back to start bleeding again. Arella reaches around with shaking hands and finds fresh blood seeping onto her shirt. She comes over dizzy and her vision starts to cloud. The sounds of voices distort and then go quiet, like she is underwater. Then silence, followed by blackness.

Chapter 7

"Nova, what did you do that for?" A muffled male voice asks.

"I did what I had to do." The female voice replies. "It was what she deserved."

"Well we can't just leave her here to die." Another male voice joins in.

"Why not? She deserves it."

"I agree." A smaller male voice joins in.

"Why are you siding with her Doahte? And how does she?" A sweet male voice says. "I'm sure it's not her fault our father and Chogan died." A slapping sound interrupts him from anything else he was going to say. "What in god's name was that for Nova? What has gotten into you." Arella can now hear crying, a horrible sound. She never liked hearing people cry, even ones who have hurt her.

"You never stick up for me!" The crying voice shouts. "Ever since you saw this thing in the forest four years ago, you have been obsessed with it."

"What do you mean?" The sweet voice asks, no confusion in his voice whatsoever.

"I saw you Nashoba, leaving the village in the dead of night. I followed you once, and do you know where I found you? Here! In the bushes, watching it."

"Stop calling her it! She has a name." Nashoba defends her.

"So what is her name?" She persists.

"Well, I don't know." Nashoba answers. "I never talked to her."

"So why did you follow her. What is it about this thing that interested you so much?" The others are completely silent. They don't know what to say.

"I don't know." Nashoba admits. "I've just never seen anyone who looks like that. And she saved us from the wolf."

"You would have been fine. You told me you had it in hand and that she just interfered." Nova spits angrily. "Did you lie to me then too?"

"Yeah okay, I lied." Nashoba admits. "What would the tribe have said if we'd told them we couldn't fend off a wolf and that a girl had done a better job on her own than we had? They would have laughed in our faces."

"Yes and so would I." Nova laughs. "You're pathetic. All of you. Not one of you deserves the title warrior."

"Now hold on a minutes Nova." Mato pipes up, his deep voice loud in the darkness. "Who are you to say that. We did our trial, and we passed. We came home safe and defeated many enemies and dangers on the way. Just because a rabid wolf caught us off guard, that's no reason to say we are not fit to be warriors." Silence follows this.

"Whatever. I'm ashamed to be your sister." Nova spits at Nashoba. "From now on I officially disown you."

Arella tries to move, but she can't. The pain in her back is overwhelming, but she can't shift her position to help. Her back feels warm, but Arella is getting cold. If she were able to move she would be shivering, but her body seems unable to do even that. She falls away into blackness again, the sounds of arguing fading into the distance.

Arella is vaguely aware of movement. Pain radiates through her back as she's bounced up and down, soft things brushing against her hands and face every now and then. "Are you sure we should have come back for them?" Arella recognises Nootau's voice. She opens her eyes, darkness still surrounds her. She is aware of pressure around her stomach.

"We couldn't just leave then to die." Nashoba answers. "Besides, she isn't heavy."

"She might not be." Mato says, although it sounds like he's struggling. "But this cat is heavy. And I have a feeling it might wake up soon." Another bump causes serious pain in Arella's back. She gasps, the noise noticed by Nashoba.

"I think this one might be waking up." He says. But with that, the pain gets too much and she falls back into blackness.

"Why did you bring her here Nashoba?" A voice asks in the darkness.

"I couldn't just leave her there, she would have died." Nashoba answers. Arella tries to move but her body does not have the strength.

"Your sister will not like this." The voice says.

"My sister can go suck an egg." Nashoba says.

"But maybe she was right." The voice starts. "I mean, it was since you said you saw this girl in the forest that things started to go wrong."

"Maybe you're right." Nashoba says. "But that doesn't mean we should let her bleed out in the forest. I thought you were better than that Hopi."

"If she really is the cause of everything bad that has happened to our tribe, I don't think she should be here." Hopi says.

"Well you don't get to make that decision. Now go get Ujarak for me. I need his help." This is the last thing Arella hears before darkness takes her again.

Arella feels like she is laid in a strange position. She feels pressure on her right hand side. "This wound on her back is deep

Nashoba." A gruff man's voice says. "I don't know if my medicines will work."

"They have to Ujarak." Nashoba pleads. "She saved my life from the wolf. I have to repay that favour." Arella hears a loud sigh.

"I will try my best young one." Ujarak replies. Arella feels more pressure, this time on her back where the wound is. "It is very deep Nashoba, and dirty." Arella feels searing pain in the wound as the healer scrapes out the dirt and grit, but she still cannot move nor open her eyes. "What did Nova do to her?"

"She knocked her out, then kicked her while she was unconscious, but this was done before that." Nashoba answers, he feels close.

"Explain child. It will keep me focused if you talk."

"We were following her, me, Nootau and Nova. I'd seen her at Chogan's funeral and followed her. I knew where she lived, I've seen her there before, but Nootau wanted to come with me, for back up. When Nova saw us leaving, she followed too, and Mato and Doahte saw her leaving and followed. They got as far as her home, where we saw her first, but they got there after the White Ghost left. We followed her and picked up her trail pretty quick, but Mato and Doahte have never been that good at tracking. They stayed by her clearing, unable to follow but not wanting to come back to the village, knowing that we would return at some point."

"Slow down Nashoba." Ujarak says in a calming voice. The pain in Arella's back becoming unbearable.

"Can she hear us?" Nashoba asks. "She twitched her face."

"No." Ujarak replies. "I have given her a powerful sedative. She will not be able to hear or feel anything." Arella laughs inwardly, but the pain does not go away. She tries to focus on Nashoba's voice.

"So we followed her trail then finally saw her. She was walking near the stream. You know, where the other tribe used to live before an invading tribe killed them all off? Anyway, there she was, kneeling by the stream. Nova was telling me I should kill her, saying it was all her fault our father died, and the it was down to her that Chogan died. I was ready to do it. I was going to shoot her with my bow. I had it aimed and everything. I would have hit her square in the back, then something caught my eye. In the distance I could see a pack of wolves." Nashoba pauses. "I thought it would be easier if I let the wolves kill her. They were going to anyway, and it would mean a meal for them." He pauses again. "That sounds awful doesn't it?"

"It does in a way." Ujarak says. "But in another light, it is the circle of life and the spirits will things that way. Better they get a meal and a kill than you taint your arrows with blood." He has finished the scraping of Arella's wound and now begins cleaning with water. This feels soothing and cool, but still a little painful. "Carry on Nashoba."

"So I lowered my bow and we watched. Nova was excited to see her torn apart by wolves, but once she got to them, she was deeply disappointed. "

"A lone wolf came out to meet the girl, smelling her scent on the wind. When he got to her, he circled her several times, then walked away. She followed and was lead back to the pack. Me, Nova and Nootau moved forwards for a better look and caught sight of her being greeted by the alpha of the pack." Ujarak stops what he's doing. "It was strange. I've never seen a wolf pack accept someone in who was not another wolf, but he did. It was then that I realized I couldn't kill her. The spirits would punish me if I did."

"I understand." Ujarak says. "This needs thinking about then." Arella feels more pressure on her back, then feels as though she is being rolled. "The wound should start to heal now. I have done all I can with it. She must not move now though for a few days."

"How do we stop her from moving?"

"We deal with that when she wakes. For now though, I want to hear about how she got that wound on her back."

"She spent a while with the wolves, then joined them on a hunt. We followed her and the pack at a distance, but Nova wanted to get closer. She still wanted me to kill the girl, and wasn't listening when I told her we couldn't. While me and Nova were arguing, the hunt began, so I missed most of it. I caught how she got hurt though." Nashoba shifts his position, getting himself comfortable. "She was standing at the edge of the herd, watching the wolves take out a buffalo when it happened. Nova snatched my bow and aimed at her. I knocked her out of the way, causing the arrow to stray. It flies towards the herd but instead of hitting the white ghost, it hits one of the buffalo. The buffalo flies into a rage and charger at her, catching her by surprise. This is how she gets hurt. Dust flies up into the air, and the next thing we see is her emerging from under its dead body covered in blood." He's getting very animated now. "I don't know how she did it, but there must be a reason she didn't die right?"

"It would make sense for the spirits to save her. Perhaps the elders will know why?" Ujarak says.

"I don't know. They like everything to be the same. They would not accept this." Nashoba thinks. "I've heard legends of a powerful being that lives in the mountains... Oh gods what was he called?" He racks his brains but cannot think. "They say he has power of the spirits and can answer any questions." Nashoba pauses to think again. "Nope, I can't remember."

"If it is meant to be that you are to visit this being, you will remember young one." Arella falls once again into darkness with this.

"What is she doing with that?!" Nova shouts, her voice so deafeningly loud that she must be right next to Arella. "That is our father's necklace!" Arella feels a sharp tug at her neck.

"I lost it in the forest the day we all met by the fire. Don't you remember? We came back and I didn't have it anymore." Nashoba replies.

"I bet she stole it, just like everything in her strange house." Nova spits.

"What do you mean Nova?" A strangers voice asks.

"The furs in her tree, and the weapons she has. There is no way they are hers. And the arrows I recognize as ours. She's a thief as well as a murderer!" Nova shouts. "Give me one good reason why I shouldn't slit her throat with her own dagger?"

"Because the spirits wouldn't allow it Nova." Ujarak says. Arella is beginning to think wherever she is, she is surrounded by strangers. She suddenly becomes very scared, surrounded by strangers with no real friend in sight. Maska! Sudden panic hits her. Last time she saw him, he was unconscious and bleeding. She tries to move again, and this time a finger twitches.

"And how wouldn't they? What makes her so special?" She snorts a laugh. "Because it certainly isn't her appearance. I mean look at her. Strange white skin, while hair, those odd purple eyes. She has bad spirits inside her, I can feel it."

"Nova this has to stop." Nashoba tries to reason with her. "Until we can prove that she did something wrong, I don't think there is anything we can do."

"But Nashoba…?"

"No Nova. I've heard enough. I want you to leave this tent now, and don't come back in here with that attitude. Oh and Nova…?"

"Yes?"

"Leave the dagger and wolf necklace behind." Nova leaves in a huff, leaving Arella in the room, unable to see and not knowing who else is in the room with her.

After a few minutes of silence, Arella can hear breathing. She wiggles her toes, slowly starting to be able to move again, careful not to move too much. She doesn't want to alert whoever is in the room with her to her being conscious. "What am I going to do?" Nashoba asks. The silence in the room tells her that she is alone with him. "I mean, you've not actually done anything wrong, but in the same way, my people need someone to blame for the bad things that have been happening. I'm worried that if I do nothing, they will come in here themselves and kill you, thinking it will change things, and I don't think it will." He sighs. "You will wake up soon, and I don't know what you will do when you wake. Ujarak says you can't hear anything, which is probably a good thing, but I wish you could hear me. I'm telling you now that I don't blame you, no matter what anyone else says, but you have to know that you're in danger. My people will kill you if they get the chance. I can't leave this tent. If I do, they will kill you. I think I can trust Nootau and Mato, but I don't know about anyone else, even Doahte. He sided with my sister without thinking. I will need to come up with a plan. We can't let you go when you wake up. If you do, my people will hunt you down, headed up by Nova, and they will kill you."

Arella opens her eyes, barely able to see through her eyelashes. She sees Nashoba, sat next to her, his head in his hands. "What do I do White Ghost?"

"Come with me to the mountain spirit." Arella answers with a rough voice. Nashoba jumps, not expecting to hear a reply from anyone.

"What?"

"Come with me to the mountain spirit" Arella says again. "The spirit will give us the answer."

"You're awake?"

"Of course I'm awake." Arella says matter of factly. "And I heard every word you've said. Including the bit about the mountain spirit." Nashoba stares at her, shocked that she is talking to him. "Please?"

"First let me ask you a question." Nashoba says.

"Anything."

"What's your name?"

"Arella."

Chapter 8

"So you want to go to the mountain?" Nashoba asks.

"It's the only way to get the approval of your tribe. Then I can live in peace with Maska without the fear of being attacked." Arella pauses, then her heart jumps. "Maska! Where is he?"

"You mean the auron cat you were with?" Nashoba asks.

"Yes, where is he?"

"Well…"

"Nashoba tell me!" Arella raises her voice and her body, causing pain to rocket through her back.

"Calm down. He's okay. We had to lock him up for our own safety though. He was ready to kill Nova, and I had to keep her safe. He broke free from the rope Nova used to tie him up and was stood over you protectively. He made it impossible for her to get to you. Unfortunately, him protecting you left him vulnerable. Nova threw rocks. Most of them missed, but before we could stop her, one hit him on the head knocking him out cold."

"We managed to get her away, kicking and screaming but we did it. By the time we got back to you, both of you were still out of it. We didn't know if you were alive or dead. You were barely breathing." Nashoba Pauses. "When we got you back here, your cat was awake. He'd have killed us all if we didn't lock him up."

"You can't lock him up." Arella is outraged.

"I can bring him to you, but you have to keep your voice down. I don't want anyone else to know you're awake yet." Arella agrees to be quiet in exchange for Maska to be brought to her.

Waiting in the tent while Nashoba fetches Maska, she looks around. This is a big tent, bigger than any she has been in before. It is made from light skins, possibly from deer but Arella cannot be sure. She has managed to sit herself up, ignoring the pain in her back as she does so. She props the furs up behind her so she can stay sat without using too many muscles. There are more furs on the floor, creating a carpet of warmth. Arella looks down at herself. She is no longer covered in the blood of the bison, and is wearing new clothes. She reaches round to her back where the buffalo's horn pierced her skin, and finds it bandaged and sore, but not bleeding through.

Outside the tent Arella can hear voices talking. There is a fire in the middle of the tent she is in, so she hadn't realised it was night outside until she looked through the gap in the doorway. Either she's been out of it for a few hours, which she doubts greatly, or she's been unconscious for more than a day. This seems like the more likely scenario. "Are you sure having her here is a good idea?" Mato asks, caution in his voice.

"I couldn't just leave her there, no matter what my sister thinks." Nashoba says. "And I feel sorry for her. She's been out in the forest on her own for... Well I don't know how long for, but it can't do anyone any good."

"Is it really our place to take her away from that though?" Nootau asks.

"What we should do is let her get back to strength, then send her back out on her own." Mato says.

"No." Nashoba says sternly. "She was clearly sent to us for a reason. We should take her to the mountain spirits, see what they say."

"Nashoba, we don't even know if they are real." Nootau objects. "For all we know, the mountain spirit is a bear that is going to tear us apart."

"You don't have to come with me, but this is something I need to do." Nashoba says. He then clearly leaves, because Arella can hear Nootau and Mato talking between themselves.

"Do you think he's doing the right thing?" Mato asks.

"I honestly don't know Mato, but I guess we have to listen to him." Nootau pauses. "He's never been wrong about anything before, and he is the future chief, so we have to listen to him. Plus, we wouldn't be being good friends if we didn't would we?"

"You have a point. Can't say I like the idea of going with a barbarian and giant cat all the way to the mountains on the other side of the lake, but I trust Nashoba." Mato replies. Arella giggles to herself, causing more pain to run through her back, but she keeps quiet. Nashoba told her to be quiet, and she will do just that.

"Plus I would follow him to the end of the earth, and I hope you would too." Mato says. "He's our brother, and we have to trust that he knows what he's doing."

"You never know…" Nootau starts. "This might lead to another adventure."

"That's the spirit." Arella hears a sound she can only imagine is Mato clapping a great hand on Nootau's back. "Let's go help Nashoba. He might need us."

Mato and Nootau's voices fade away into the distance. They've been called away to help Nashoba bring Maska to Arella. "Barbarian. Ha!" Arella laughs. "What made them think I'm a barbarian? Could be that I was covered in blood I guess." She looks down at her clean clothes. "Nice clothes though!" She lifts her arms from under the furs. They're bare, and she can see dark purple bruising on the top of her right arm. Arella looks to the table next to her, finding a bucket of water. She leans over and looks at her reflection. A black eye takes up most of her face, a deep gash over her eyebrow, clean and sewn but visible. "Nova took another go at you after she'd already knocked you unconscious." Nashoba says as he enters the tent, seeing Arella looking shocked at her own reflection.

Behind him comes Mato and Nootau, carrying a heavy wooden cage with a very angry auron cat inside, growling and hissing at his captors.

"Maska!" Arella cries out in joy. "Please let him out of there, he doesn't like it." She pleads.

"No way am I letting it out." Nootau argues.

"Nootau, do it." Nashoba orders.

"But..."

"Nootau!" He reluctantly opens the cage door, and although Maska growls at him, he does not make a move towards any of the men in the tent. He simply jumps up onto Arella's bed, lying himself across her legs, purring loudly as she strokes his back. Looking protectively over Arella, the end of his tail wagging angrily, his ears pinned back against his head. Arella can see the wound on his head, and the lump that Nova's last rock must have caused. She rubs his head gently, knowing it's hurt him. She makes a mental note to take a good look at his head if it looks to be bothering him.

"Good boy Maska." Arella praises him. Nashoba relaxes and sits on the edge of Arella's bed, but the other two stand further away. "I'm surprised Maska is letting you sit this close." Arella observes.

"Maybe he likes me." Nashoba brags.

"Or maybe he just doesn't see you as a threat." Arella laughs. Mato sighs.

"Down to business then." Nootau says. "When do we set off for the mountain?"

"Cool it Nootau." Nashoba laughs. "I think she might need a little more time to heal before we can go anywhere."

"Well how long does it take for you to get better?" Nootau presses.

"How long would it take you to recover from a buffalo horn in your back." Arella laughs. "It will take me as long as it would take any of you." She grabs a handful of hair and holds it in the air. "Just because my hair and skin are different, doesn't mean I'm magic or something."

"So a few weeks then?" Mato asks.

"I'd say so yeah, then I will be able to move."

Nootau pulls Nashoba to the side. "We can't have her here for that long. Nova and the others will get suspicious. And we will have to be guarding her the whole time. It's a waste of resources and time."

"But what else can we do Nootau? This is something I need to do. I think she was sent to us for a reason, and she was wearing this when we found her." Nashoba holds up the red wolf necklace. "This was my fathers, it has to mean something right?"

"Nova would say because she was a thief." Nootau says. This hurts Arella. She can hear every word they are saying, and Mato has noticed this. He just watches her, listening to Nootau and Nashoba talk.

"But what do you truly think Nootau?" Nashoba asks.

"I think…" He pauses, looking over Nashoba's shoulder at the strange white girl in the middle of the tent, purple eyes wide with worry and anger. "Oh sod it! Let's take a risk. Like you said, it must be for a reason."

"So it's settled then." Nashoba says, intending everyone in the tent to hear. "We help Arella get back on her feet, then to the mountains to see the mountain spirit."

"Arella?" Mato questions.

"Yeah." Arella answers. "I have a name other than the White Ghost you know." Then she laughs, causing more pain in her back.

"Well yeah we knew you would. It's just…" Nootau starts.

"It's just what?" Arella asks.

"We didn't expect you to be so normal." Arella laughs again, jolting in discomfort. Maska shifts his position, uncomfortable at Arella being in pain.

"Okay. I think it's time we let Arella rest." Nashoba says.

"I'm okay really." Arella insists.

"No it's okay. We're going." Mato says. "Nashoba, do you want us to bring anything back later?"

"Some food might be nice?"

"I don't know how easy it will be. Nova's in control of that at the moment." Nootau replies.

"Tell them I asked for it. Then they'll have to." Mato and Nootau nod in agreement then leave the tent. Nashoba gets up too.

"Are you leaving as well?" Arella asks.

"Just for a little while. I have things I need to do." He answers. He looks at the worry on Arella's face. "I won't be gone for long, and Mato and Nootau are keeping an eye on the tent. Plus, you have that auron cat of yours to protect you." He ruffles the top of Maska's head. The great cat purrs loudly. Arella looks at Nashoba, shocked.

"I'm surprised he's letting you get close to him."

"Why is that?"

"Maska tends to hide from people, and he's been hurt bad by people in the past. He usually only trusts me." Arella strokes the long fur on Maska's back, remembering that he really needs brushing as she gets her fingers caught in a matt. "But he must trust you, and that's reason enough for me to trust you."

"You trust his judgement that much?" Nashoba asks.

"Why not? What better than animal intuition?" Arella smiles. "When you've lived like I have for the last few years, you learn to pick up on the little things, and the main thing I picked up is that Maska is never wrong about something. If he feels uncomfortable or scared, I know something is wrong." Nashoba considers this for a while.

"I guess this makes sense." He stops stroking Maska's head and gets up, walking towards the door of the tent. "Get some sleep. I'll be back soon." He leaves the tent, leaving Arella and Maska alone in a strange tent surrounded by dangers and strangers.

"I wonder where he's going." Arella says out loud, only Maska to hear her. He turns and looks at her, his different coloured eyes shining in the light on the fire. "I know what you're thinking Maska, we're not safe here. But what choice do we have. You're hurt, and I'm not better. We will stay until we are better, then leave the village." She pauses. "I want to go see the mountain spirit though Maska." He glares at her. "I knew you wouldn't like it. But it's something I have to do Maska." He grumbles in complaint. "Come on Maska. I have to know what this spirit says. He might know why I am how I am, and how I fit into this world." Maska turns away from Arella. "You don't have to come if you don't want to though. I can look after myself." Maska drops his head to his legs, not looking at Arella. She knew telling him this would make him angry, he doesn't want to see her in danger, but she has to find out who she is, and Nashoba can help her do it. Arella also knows that there is no way Maska will make her go on her own, he will go with her, albeit reluctantly.

Arella closes her eyes, allowing herself to relax a little. She knows that Maska will protect her, and she has faith that the spirits would not allow her to die for no reason. They're leading her down this past for a reason, and who is she to argue with them. The vibration of Maska's purring really relaxes her, and with a smile on her face, Arella falls into a deep dreamless sleep.

Chapter 9

Arella opens her eyes, the dull light of the rising sun lighting the inside of the tent. It feels strange waking up somewhere you do not know. It's been a long time since Arella has woken up in a strange place, and she doesn't like the feeling. The most un-nerving part is not knowing how the creatures around her are going to act. In the forest, Arella knows what every animal will do, where they will go. Here, she has no clue, and this frightens her. The fire in the tent has now gone out, but it's warmth can still be felt. Maska still sleeps on Arella's legs, keeping her safe. Outside, loud voices can be heard. It must have been what woke her. "I can't believe you Nashoba!" It's Nova's voice Arella can hear. Her head hurts where Nova kicked her. Maska jumps awake at the sound of her voice also. He growls low.

"Hush Maska, I want to hear what they're saying." Arella whispers. Maska quietens, but the end of his tail continues to flick.

"Nova Calm down." Mato tries.

"No!" She shouts again, this time louder. "How dare you bring that murderer back here when I specifically asked you to leave it under the tree to die where it belongs!"

"I couldn't just leave her Nova." Nashoba answers. "She…"

"It's not a she Nashoba. It doesn't deserve that. It's a murderer and a freak, end of story. And I want it out!" She yells. More whispers and words can be heard from outside the tent. The argument must have woken everyone in the village up. Now everyone in the village knows she's there. This could get very dangerous, very fast.

"Nova, she has a name, and she is not a murderer."

"Sticking up for your precious White ghost again I see Nashoba." She spits.

"Nova enough." Nootau tries.

"Oh don't you start too." She laughs. "You're all as bad as each other." Arella half wishes she could see what was going on outside the tent, to see who exactly was out there. Arella moves in her bed. She can't just lay here while this is going on. They clearly don't want her here, and it's not in her nature to stay where she isn't wanted. That's the entire reason she left her tribe in the first place.

The pain in her back is easing, but it still hurts to move. Arella gets up from her bed, closely followed by Maska. She moves over to the side of the tent, collecting her cloak from a peg made form deers antlers, now no longer covered in blood, but dry. The hole in the back a stark reminder of the buffalo Arella fought only the day before. She pulls it onto her shoulders, tying it at the front, lifts the hood up onto her head and picks up her weapons. They were laid at the foot of the bed, just outside her field of view. She pulls her boots on then pauses to listen to the argument still raging on outside. Arella creeps to the side of the tent where the arguing is coming from. She moves a piece of tent, peeking outside. Careful not to be spotted, Arella watches the argument.

"I forbid you from going anywhere with that creature!" Nova yells.

"You can't tell me what to do Nova. You're not our mother!" Nashoba yells back. All Arella can think, listening to the siblings fight, it the guilt she feels. If she had only stayed away from Nashoba and the other men when she'd seen them in the forest all those years ago, none of this would be happening. T.here is so much anger on Nova's face. It's twisted into an ugly shape

Arella picks up her grathon and, using it for added balance, ducks out of the back of the tent and away from the arguing. As she leaves the village, Maska at her side, the arguing dies away. She makes her way into the forest she knows so well, her sanctuary, and starts the long walk back home.

The morning due on the ground makes walking difficult, and not having the full strength in her back makes it even harder. Maska walks close to Arella, helping her stay on her feet as they move.

There is no fog this morning. The temperature in the air warmer than it has been for the last few days. Arella is thankful for this. Frost was threatening to creep in, and the last thing she wants right now is ice to fall on. From years living in the wild, Arella has come to realise that cold makes wounds hurt more, and they tend to take longer to heal

The tangle of roots beneath her feet threaten to trip Arella up. She stays stead on her feet, but the effort of this is draining. She is not paying attention to anything that is happening around her. She does not see the colours of the autumn leaves as they change from green to orangey brown, nor does she see the motto deer that flee from her and Maska as they move through the tree. She doesn't see the rabbits who scamper back into their dens, nor the frogs on the ground, taking full advantage of the damp leaf litter. She simply plods on, supported by her bloodglass grathon and her feline companion Maska. The air around her swirls and spirals. The colours blending together, becoming one big blur in Arella's vision. Through half closed eyes, Arella watches her home land pass by, unconscious threatening to take her over. She fights with the blackness all the way home, and the pain in her back becoming so painful it brings tears to her purple eyes, the stinging from the stitches still fresh.

The forest is almost silent on the way back from the village, only the morning calls of a few lonely birds. It is fully light by the time Arella and Maska make their way back to their home, and Arella is exhausted.

As they enter the clearing, Arella is shocked by what she sees. "No." She gasps. "How could she?" It looks as though when Arella was unconscious, Nova did her best to ruin her home. The tiredness and pain that gripped her just a few minutes ago, now replaces by anger and confusion. The chicken pen has been broken, but no immediate sign of them. Arella moves over to the pen and finds a clear small boot print on the ground where the weaved vines have been broken, confirming that Nova broke it. A few feathers are stuck to the broken vines. When Arella takes a closer look inside the pen, her worst fears come to life. The lifeless body of one of her hens lies broken on the floor of the pen, covered in its own blood. Another lies further back in the pen, and feathers strewn everywhere. Arella drops to her knees, pulling the lifeless body of the chicken into her arms. "How could she?" Arella drops the chicken to the floor again. "The foxes got to them Maska." She says as she turns to look at the auron cat. He stares at her, his big green and yellow eyes wide with emotion.

Arella surveys the rest of her home. Many of her bushes have been flattened, and the berries squished into the ground. A few of the bigger bushes look like they might make it through, but most of them are gone, purple and red stain the floor, leaves and broken branches litter the ground, the destruction clear to see. Dropping to her knees, not quite believing what she is seeing with her own eyes, Arella begins to cry. All the work she put into her home has been a waste.

Arella looks towards her treehouse. This has escaped damage, being far too big and well build. Thank the gods for that, but everything else is ruined. A voice from behind her makes Arella jump. "Wow, this place is a mess." It's Nashoba. Fury fills Arella, and the pain in her back is forgotten. She shouts at him, finger pointing in his direction, clear anger on her face as she turns on his, getting shakily to her feet.

"What are you doing here?"

"You left." Nashoba starts confused. "I wanted to make sure you're okay."

"Ha!" Arella laughs. "Yeah, I'm absolutely fine." She swings her arms wide open, causing her hood to fall down. "Just my entire food supply for the winter has been destroyed, and the person who did it knows exactly where I live." Nashoba doesn't know quite what to say to this. "What am I going to do now?" Arella asks, although she doesn't wait for an answer. She walks around, turning her back on Nashoba and takes off her cloak. She hangs it on one of the low branches of her treehouse. "I've spent the last four years building this place, getting it safe, secure and with enough food to last me and Maska over the winter. No one knew where I was, and I was happy." She turns to look at him again. "Then you come along and ruin it."

"I didn't do anything." Nashoba argues, sadness in his eyes.

"Not directly no. But you brought your sister here when you followed me, and she did this." Arella says, swinging her arms out to emphasise her point.

"Hang on a minute…" Nashoba contests. "It was you who followed me back to the village. It was you who was at the funeral. I only followed you back from there. And I can't help it if my nosey sister followed me."

"But she did. And now I have to leave my home, move far away and start again. Just when I was comfortable and safe." Tears begin to form in Arella's eyes. Arella turns away so Nashoba won't see them. She is tired and weak and unable to deal with emotions at the moment. "Just leave."

"I'm not going anywhere." Nashoba says stubbornly. "Not with you like this."

"Why." Arella turns back to face him, a single tear falling from her violet eyes. "What good will you do here? Everything is already ruined, and I will no doubt be killed in my sleep if I don't move quickly."

"But you can't leave." Nashoba tries.

"Why not? There is nothing here for me now!" Arella is gettitting far too worked up.

"Because we're going to the mountain spirit for answers."

"Why would you want to go anywhere with me? All I do is cause suffering."

"Because I have questions too." Nashoba starts. "And how do you mean, all you do is cause suffering?"

"Well look what happens when I go anywhere. In my old tribe, every time I joined in at a party, someone died or got very ill. Since I came to the forest and saw you, Nootau, Mato and Doahte practising, your father has died, and now that young man who was to be married to your sister. My own mother died because of me." More tears escape Arella's eyes.

"None of that can have been your fault." Nashoba tries to comfort Arella. Defeated she sits herself down on the floor in front of the white treehouse, causing pain to ricochet through her back. Maska sits himself down close to her, trying to comfort her with his purring. "Your mother dying can't have been because of you. How did she die, might I ask?" Nashoba moves to sit in front of Arella.

"I'd rather not talk about it." Arella says.

"Well I'm not giving you a choice." He says. "Come on. Tell me everything." His inquisitiveness intrigues Arella. Why is he so interested in her? Why does he care. She's suspicious, but she has nothing to lose from telling him.

"I never met my mother, nor my father. I've been told I was conceived in a raid on my village, as my mother fell pregnant with me soon after. I was born, and my mother died. Not much more to say on it than that." Arella finishes, brushing the remaining tears from her cheeks, the water no longer falling.

"There must be more to your story than that?" Nashoba eggs her on. "What about your childhood, what your tribe was like? Anything so I know more about you."

"But why do you want to know?" Arella asks. "Why do you even care where I came from, or what my life has been like? What do I matter to you?" Arella is really struggling to comprehend why she would mean enough to Nashoba for him to care where she came from and who she is. Nobody has ever talked to her, not really, and nobody had ever cared about anything she had said. It was a strange feeling to have someone talking to her. "Okay, so I have two choices. I can either shut off the first person who has every given a damn about me and cared about what I have to say, go my own way with Maska and be lonely again, or I can give it a go, talk to him and see where it leads me." Arella thinks for a little while, then she has her answer. "Let's go for it. What's the worst that could happen?"

Before she starts, Arella decides she should get comfortable, and make Nashoba comfortable too, they might be there a while. "Maska? Could you do me a huge favour?" The great auron cat raises his head, the purring continues. "Could you go up into the treehouse and bring down the furs? I don't think I can get up today." Maska lifts his huge body from the ground and does just this, emerging from the treehouse with all of the furs in his mouth. Arella attttempts to get up from her spot on the ground, but the pain in her face is clearly visible. Nashoba gets to his feet and offers her a hand up. Arella looks at him suspiciously, she still does not trust him completely. She takes his hand and he helps her up. Much less painful than getting up herself.

Arella moves over to the ground hut. This has also stayed intact after Nova's little rampage. Arella is thankful for that. This will be her bed for the next few days, until her back has healed enough for her to climb into the treehouse, or until she leaves her home completely. Arella positions the furs along the back wall of the hut. She looks up to ask Maska to bring her the cloak, but finds Nashoba already holding it in front of her. "I think you might need a new cloak." He remarks.

"I made that myself I'll have you know." She smiles, proud of her work. She looks at the hole in the back. "But you might be right." Nashoba hands it to her, and Arella pulls the cloak over her shoulders.

Nashoba looks around the ground hut with excited eyes. "Did you build this place all by yourself?" He asks.

"It's taken a while to get right." Arella says as she builds up a fire. "But yeah, I've built it myself."

"I have to say I'm impressed." Nashoba says. He moves to sit in the hut with Arella and Maska, who has already positioned himself close to her.

"Before you sit down, could you do me a favour?" Arella asks. "I'd ask Maska but I don't entirely trust him." Maska growls low at this. "Oh hush you."

"What is it?"

"Could you climb up into the tree and fetch a deer leg down? I'm starving, and it needs cooking off before it goes off." She asks. Nashoba does as she asks and a few minutes later returns with the leg.

"That's a pretty cool treehouse." He says as he sits down on the opposite side to Arella as Maska. "Must have taken you ages to build."

"Only a couple of weeks."

"And it is water tight?"

"I have used animal skins like in the tents to make it so yeah. Wouldn't be much good as a home if it let water in."

"True." Nashoba answers. He really does seem interested in Arella's home.

"It's just a shame I have to leave it." Arella says. She is sad about that. Not really angry anymore.

"Maybe you don't have to." Nashoba says.

"What do you mean?"

"Maybe we can convince everyone in my tribe that you aren't bad, and that your nothing to be feared." Nashoba is excited by this. "Then maybe you and Maska could stay here."

"That would be nice Nashoba, but I don't think it will happen." Arella is unsure of this idea.

"We will make it happen." Nashoba is determined. "All we need to do is go see the mountain spirit. We will take Nootau and Mato, they believe us. Then they can back us up when the mountain spirit explains everything."

"I'm willing to try is you are."

"That's settled then. We will go to the mountain spirit as soon as you are able." Nashoba shuffles to get more comfortable as Arella brings the fire in front of her to life. "And until then, I will stay with you to keep you safe."

"Why does Nashoba want to keep me safe?" Arella wonders. *"What would he gain from it? And why is he being so protective of me?"*

Chapter 10

With a warm fire burning in front of her, the leg of the motto deer cooking away above it, and Maska chomping away on the bone of another, Arella begins telling Nashoba about her childhood and her life.

"When my mother died, I was taken in by another member of the tribe, Nayleen. She'd just lost a child a few months before, and she was good friends with my mother. She was without a husband, and very lonely." Arella turns the deer leg, making sure it doesn't catch on one side and burn. "She brought me up, and she was wonderful at it, really she was, but the others in the tribe still didn't like me. They thought that I killed my mother when I was born, and they always told me I did."

"So, not meaning to sound horrible, but why didn't they just kill you when you were born? If they thought you were bad luck, and that you'd killed your mother, why didn't they leave you out in the wild to die of something?" Nashoba asks.

"They believed that the spirits send us things for a reason, and that they send troubles and bad things our way to test us. I guess they thought I was one of those things, and that killing me would bring them even worse luck than they were already getting." Arella laughs at herself.

"Why are you laughing, that's horrible." Nashoba says.

"Because it's funny really." Arella laughs again. "by driving me out of the tribe and making me feel like I was not wanted there, they came across the worst luck they have ever had."

"And what would that be?" Nashoba is interested. Arella turns the leg again. She then takes her dagger, pierces the flesh and peeks inside. It is still very pink, a little too rare for her to eat.

"Well, about two years after I left the tribe, I went back to the village, just to have a look, to see what was happening there. I've heard a lot of noise the night before, and I was curious. By the time I got to the edge of the forest, I could tell something wasn't right. There was smoke rising into the sky, white but a lot of it. I followed the stream along the way to where the village was, but there wasn't much left." Arella coughs, black smoke from her own fire caught in her throat. "There were bodies on the floor, all covered in blood, and a lot of things had gone. All that was left was the tents, and the bodies of the villagers. I can only assume they were hit by a raiding party." She laughs again. "Sorry, I shouldn't be laughing. It's just, I never realised how stupid they all were."

"What do you mean?"

"Well... What kind of person thinks that setting up the village in the middle of an open plain where you are easily visible from others is a good idea. And get this. They thought that the forest was a dangerous place to be, and that they would die if they went in there."

"So that's the tribe you came from?" Nashoba asks.

"Yeah why?"

"Because they really were the most cowardly people I have ever seen." Nashoba says. "My father used to tell me stories about how stupid they were." Nashoba suddenly becomes sad. "My father…"

"Do you want to talk about it?" Arella asks.

"I've not really talked to anyone about him." Nashoba says.

"It's okay." Arella reassures him. "You don't have to talk if you don't want to."

"Thank you." Nashoba smiles a sad smile. "Tell me more then. What made you come into the forest?"

"I've always liked it here." Arella says looking up at the roof of her ground hut. "And it was away from my village. Plus, I hate the sun."

"What do you mean you hate the sun?" Nashoba is confused. "The sun gives us life."

"It also burns." Arella states. "You wouldn't know. You have lovely dark skin. But me… Well when your skin is this pale, the sun doesn't like it. I burn easy, and the light of the sun makes it hard to see. I thought coming into the forest would help with that."

"Has it?"

"Definitely." Arella smiles. "It was the best decision I ever made."

Silence falls over them for a little while. Arella has pretty much forgotten about the pain in her back, the wound not bothering her at all. The silence they sit in, only broken by Maska's purring and snoring, is not uncomfortable at all. Arella does not feel that she needs to fill the filence with words, and Nashoba does not look like he is struggling for something to say. His green eyes seem to shimmer I the light of the fire, the flames bringing out the fellow hews in them. *"I could stare into those eyes forever."* Then Arella thinks of something else she can talk about, something she is rather proud of. "I don't know if you'll remember, it might have been while you were away."

"What is it?"

"Do you remember, about four years ago, there were a bunch of animals turning up in the forest with poison arrows embedded in their bodies?"

"I remember a few yeah, then I left. The others in my tribe said that we had a huge thunder storm then it all stopped." Nashoba says. "Why, what about it?"

"It was me who stopped it." Arella says proudly. Maska growls lightly. "And Maska too, he helped."

"What do you mean it was you?" Nashoba asks. "How could you have stopped it. You were only what, thirteen?"

"Fifteen actually, but it's true. We stopped them from killing all of the animals."

"Stopped who?"

"Well. It was how I came across Maska actually."

"That was a question I was going to ask." Nashoba says. His green eyes bright with excitement. He shuffles a little where he sits, getting more comfortable for the story Arella is going to tell. His expression when he speaks is very animated, making Arella think of a small child being told a bedtime story. "I've wanted to know how he came to be your companion since I saw you and him fight together in my village."

"I woke up one night hearing a horrible sound, and it turned out to me Maska's mother. She'd been hit with an arrow and was passing through my clearing. I followed her to her den, which is a good half days walk away. There… long story short… I had to end her life, and Maska came under my protection. He grew up fast living we me, and quickly became nearly adult sized. In the few months we were together, we noticed that more and more animals had poison arrows in them. I took it upon myself to end their suffering but decided it couldn't carry on. So when Maska was old enough, we set out to find the people that were doing it."

"We found their trail and followed it for a few days. We found them, or more to the point, they found us. They kidnapped Maska and threatened to kill us too. Really nutty people. A woman with a wolf skull on her head, and three brothers, one with a goat skull, one with a bison skull and one with foxes skulls. Something about killing animals so she could have a baby. Really really insane. Long story short, Me, Maska and a pack of wolves killed them. Although I didn't get any blood on my hands, Maska did a fine job. I was very proud of him for that." Arella ruffles Maska's head. She turns the leg again, checking to see how well done it is.

"How did you get the wolves to help you?" Nashoba asks.

"I'm not entirely sure." Arella admits. "We got to the point with them where I thought we were both going to die, I really did. Then out of nowhere, a pack of wolves came from behind and finished them off. I couldn't watch though, too much blood for me. The noise will stay with me forever though." Arella looks off into the distance, lost in thought. Nashoba is desperately trying to think of something to take her mind off it.

"So tell me from your point of view about when you saved us from that rabid wolf." Nashoba urges. This works.

"I was watching you, Nootau, Mato and Doahte from a tree, with Maska beside me, although he was only a kitten then. I was watching you fire arrows for hours." Nashoba looks confused.

"How could you just be watching for hours without getting bored." This is a statement rather than a question. Nashoba wouldn't have the patience to sit in the same place watching someone do something he would want to be doing himself.

"The reason I watched you all so much was to teach myself how to fight, how to use a bow, how to look after myself." Arella admits, blushing a little.

"Well it clearly worked."

"I don't know." Arella argues, feeling the deep wound on her back. "Anyway, I'd been watching for hours, and I was going to leave, then I saw it. I saw the eyes first, then his snarling white teeth. You hadn't seen it yet, and I didn't know how to warn you without giving myself away. So I waited, hoping you would see it, but you didn't. Not until it was on top of you. The rest is a bit of a blur really. I remember its eyes and the hungry look on its face, the saliva dripping from open jaws, but then the next thing I remember is seeing thousands of bees and shouting to get your attention then hiding." Arella is looking deep into Nashoba's eyes now, the emerald green mesmerising.

"Well thank you." Arella blushes and looks down. Nashoba catches her chin with his hand and lifts it up. "No I mean it. Without you we would probably be dead, or at least missing a leg or two." Arella laughs at this, her cheeks hot with embarrassment. She is still looking into Nashoba's eyes, and he's looking into hers. He smiles, a nervous smile and leans towards her.

A sudden crack of a branch makes them jump, and Maska gets up from his place next to Arella, his ears pricked up, listening. "What's up with him?" Nashoba asks, clearly a little annoyed at being interrupted.

"Probably heard a rabbit or something." Arella says unsure. "I hope it's not Nova following me again." She thinks. Maska trots off into the clearing. Arella, with the help of Nashoba, gets to her feet and walks out into the clearing herself. Maska has walked into the bushes. The pain in Arella's back is there again, dull and in the background, but still there. Rustling in the bushes, Maska's found whatever was making the noises. He growls, then stops. His silence is a little un-nerving. "Maska?"

"Mato it's going to eat me." Nootau's voice can be heard.

"Don't be silly Nootau, it's not going to… Ow." Mato's loud voice sounds, as a loud thump rumbles through the trees. "Bloody thing knocked me over." Arella is laughing hard now.

"Maska come here." She shouts to the auron cat. "Stop knocking people over. It's impolite." Maska emerges from the bushes, tail high in the air, a catty grin on his face.

Nootau and Mato also come out from the cover of the bushes, looking very sheepish. "What are you two doing in there?" Nashoba asks. "Were you following me again?"

"You disappeared. We didn't know where you'd gone." Nootau starts.

"What did you think had happened to me?" Nashoba questions.

"Well we thought…"

"You thought what?"

"We don't know what we thought. But we had to come looking for you." Nootau replies.

"Well I'm clearly fine." Nashoba is annoyed. "So you can go now."

"They don't have to go anywhere Nashoba." Arella says. "They can stay. There'f plenty of food for everyone, and I'd like to get to know them better."

"What for?" Nashoba asks.

"If they're going to come to the mountains with us, I want to get to know them." Nashoba isn't so sure. "Plus when you think about it. It means more people to keep watch, and more people to keep me safe." Nashoba reluctantly agrees.

"Okay, but if anything happens, I swear to the gods I'm not to blame."

"I take full responsibility." Arella says, bowing slightly, causing more pain in her back. "Now can we please go and eat before the motto deer burns and goes horrible?"

So the four of them and Maska move back into the ground hut. Arella and Nashoba exchange nervous glances, sitting apart with Maska in the middle.

Arella pulls her bloodglass dagger from her boot, making Nootau jump at the sudden movement. Arella giggles at this. She begins stripping slices off the deer leg and handing them out to people. As Arella hands Nashoba his piece, their fingers touch, causing her to jump a little with the heat. The others don't notice this.

"So where did you get your weapons from?" Nootau asks, his mouth already full of meat.

"When I left my old tribe to come live in the forest, I cleared out my old tent." Arella says taking a bite of her strip of meat. "The tent was the one my adopted mother and I lived in, but I never went through her things when she died. The weapons were ducked away inside a doeskin bag, and I'd not found them till I cleared the tent out." She picks up the dagger and hands it, hilt first, to Nootau. "Here take a look, but be careful, it's very sharp." He takes the dagger.

"Very light isn't it?" He says.

"The lightest thing I've ever held yeah. But it's extremely strong. Can cut through bone." Arella states. Nootau hands the dagger to Mato who inspects it too. He then hands it to Nashoba.

"It's beautiful." He then hands it back to Arella, who uses it to slice another strip of meat for everyone.

"As well as the dagger, in the bag I found were arrow heads and a grathon." Nashoba, Nootau and Mato all look at her confused. "A grathon is like a spear, but double ended. I use mine mainly for fishing, but I believe they were used a lot in ancient times for fighting and hunting."

"What of the arrow heads though?" Nashoba asks.

"I never managed to fit them to my arrows. Every time I tried, the arrows would not fly straight." Arella looks defeated.

"Maybe I could have a go?" Nootau asks. "I'm usually quite good at making arrows." Arella beams a beautiful smiles a beautiful smile under the purple bruising on her face.

"That would be amazing." She says. Arella jumps up from her seat I the ground hut, taking the bloodglass arrow heads from their safe place in the hollow. She picks up the arrows too, the makeshift stone heads looking tatty. She brings them back to the ground hut, disturbing Maska on her way back to her seat. She hands Nootau the arrows and bloodglass heads. "Thank you for doing this." Arella gushes. "No rush though."

"Don't thank me till I've made them." He examines the bloodglass heads. "Ans the have to fly straight." The light from the fire catches on the shining arrow head.

"They really are beautiful." Nashoba says. Arella looks up and finds him looking at her. She blushes and quickly starts eating again to take the pressure off his green eyed stare.

They eat in silence for a minute or two before Nashoba strikes up conversation again. "Please tell me you made sure my sister wasn't following you again." He says to Mato and Nootau.

"Oh she's far too busy to follow us anywhere." Nootau sniggers.

"Why, what's she doing?" Nashoba asks.

"Oh you don't want to know." Nootau teases.

"Yes I do, tell me." Nashoba is starting to get angry.

"She's with Doahte." Mato admits.

"What do you mean she's with him?" Nashoba is mad.

"Turns out it didn't take her long to get over Chogan." Nootau laughs.

"It's not funny Nootau." Nashoba is mad. "I can't believe she would do this."

"Nashoba calm down." Mato tries to calm him. "She could be with someone worse."

"It's not that." Nashoba explains. "I knew there was something going on with them. I just didn't know what." Arella can't quite believe what she's hearing.

"So you're telling me, she ruined my home, nearly killed Maska and beat me up when I was unconscious for no good reason, because the person she was doing it all for didn't really mean anything to her?" She asks, stunned.

"I guess so yeah." Mato answers.

"Well isn't that just a brilliant addition to a crappy day?" Arella says, clearly annoyed by this. "I normally don't hold grudges." She says. "But that's going to be hard to let go of."

"Tell me about it." Nashoba agrees. Arella is seething, blood boiling in her veins. She looks over at Nashoba, his emerald eyes sad. Al her anger dissipates. Now all Arella feels is sadness for him. He feels betrayed by his sister, and there's nothing she can do to comfort him. She throws him a smile in an attempt to cheer him up. The corner of his mouth turns up, a small smile returned.

Chapter 11

The next morning, Arella wakes up confused. Once again, she is not in the comfort of her treehouse, but instead in the ground hut. Although most of the smells are familiar, she is in the wrong place. She is covered with the furs she normally sleeps with, and Maska is laid behind her, keeping her warm, but there are others with her. Partially familiar snores, breathing and smells are sleeping close to Arella. She cannot see any of their faces, but knows she knows them from somewhere. She lays on the ground, racking her brain, trying to remember who they are. Why is this so hard? Should she just remember. Then it hits her. Nashoba, Nootau and Mato stayed with her last night. She smiles as she looks at their sleeping faces. Has she made friends? At last does someone other than Maska care about her?

In the dim morning light, with fog and mist surrounding her Arella realises something. "Gods I was stupid." Arella says out loud, causing the men around her to stir a little. She hushes herself, not wanting to wake anyone. She moves from where she was sleeping, trying not to hurt her back as she moves, but staying as quiet as possible. She moves away from the group of men sleeping in the ground hut, Mato snoring loud. "I wonder how I even slept through that."

Arella whispers to herself. Watching her auron cat companion, laid on his back, long gangly legs in the air, his mouth hanging open, his pink belly exposed. Arella has to stifle a laugh at the sight. The men are all facing the centre except for Nashoba, he is facing the entrance to the hut, keeping watch, or he was until he fell asleep. She looks at his face, relaxed when he sleeps, his features soft. "Come on Arella, stay focused." She tells herself.

In the night, Arella had a thought, and she can't believe she didn't think of it sooner. Barrow berries. They worked to cure poison all those years ago, so surely they will help with her back. She can hardly believe she almost forgot about them. Arella looks around her clearing, desperate to find the berries. The faster she finds them, the faster she can be better, the faster she can go to the mountains, talk to the mountain spirit and find out why she is the way she is.

A voice behind her startles Arella. "Why are you up do early?" It's Nashoba. Of course it's Nashoba. She jumps at his voice, but hopes he does not see this. She recovers herself quickly, calming her quickened heartbeat.

"Looking for barrow berries." She answers. He stares at her blankly.

"What for?" He asks.

"They might help with my back." She answers. Clearly thinking Nashoba should know this.

"Why would they help with your back? Do they take pain away or something?" Arella turns to look at him, not sure if Nashoba is joking or being serious. The look on his face tells her it is the later.

"Oh come on. Tell me you know this one."

"Know what?" Nashoba asks, a little annoyed at Arella not answering his question.

"Oh you really don't know." Arella says. "Wow. I thought it's something everyone knew."

"What Arella, what is it?"

"Barrow berries have healing properties." She states. Nashoba looks at her in shock.

"No way."

"It's true." Arella says. "And I can't believe you didn't know it already. It's been ages since I've had to use them, not since Wolf and her disciples, but they work well. It might not heal me completely, but it will at least start the process so I can start training again."

"What do you mean training?" Nashoba asks.

"I like to run, but I need to do it a lot to keep my fitness up, and this will have set me back big-time. I also need to practice my aim with shooting, or that will go off target too."

"But you were an amazing shot the other day at our village." Nashoba says. "You could probably teach us a thing or two." He gestures behind himself to the others still sleeping. Maska yawns lazily, opens his green eye to find Arella and sees her standing with Nashoba. He yawns again, showing his big white teeth, the closes his lazy eye again and goes back to sleep, clearly not worried about her being with him.

"Maybe, but my hand to hand combat is lacking." Arella admits.

"Maybe I can help with that?" Nashoba suggests.

"Really? Would you?" Arella is excited. This is exactly what she wanted, someone to learn to fight from. She can't help but beam a smile. She must look ridiculous and like a small child who's just been told they were going to be the most important person in the world.

"I'll help you learn to fight, if you can help get my aim up to scratch. Deal?" Nashoba holds his hand out for Arella to shake. She's never done this before, and isn't quite sure what to do. She looks at the hand, a puzzled expression on her face. "Take my hand and shake it Arella." Arella. Nashoba said her name. It sounds like birds singing in the soft spring wind Like flowers in a meadow, just beautiful. She loves it when he says her name. She takes his strong hand, the warmth of his skin penetrating hers, making her stomach dance uncontrollably. She can feel her cheeks getting warmer again and turns away. "Thank the gods for the bruising on my face. It's hiding my embarrassment." She thinks. Arella gets down on the ground.

"Will you help me look for them?" Arella asks. "I had a few bushes with them growing on in this area. Most of them are gone now, but there should still be some."

"How many do we need?" Nashoba asks as he gets down on the ground with Arella.

"As many as you can find." She answers.

Arella's back pain is becoming unbearable towards the end of their search, but by the time her and Nashoba have finished collecting berries, they have a good couple of handfuls each in a pile on the floor. By this time, Maska is up and wide awake. "Maska do me a favour?" Arella asks the giant auron cat without even turning. She knew he was right behind her without seeing him. He blinks at her. "Go up into the house and get me one of the giant shells?" Maska does this, returning with the biggest shell Nashoba has ever seen.

"Where did you find that?" He asks.

"There are loads of them on the bottom of the lake, with little fleshy animals inside. They taste kind of nasty, but it's one of the new things I found to eat in my first winter here." Arella then takes the shell from Maska and starts putting the berries into it.

"How did you know Maska was behind you?" Nashoba questions.

"I know the sound of his breathing, and the way he walks." Arella explains. "I've known him for the last four years. Spending that amount of time with someone makes you in tune with them. Don't you feel that way with them?" She gestures to Mato and Nootau, both mock fighting in the clearing.

"I guess I see what you're saying." He agrees, smiling at her.

By the edge of the lake, Arella sits and mashes the berries up into a thick paste. "Damn!" She says through gritted teeth as one of the berries flies out of the shell and onto the floor.

"Are they still frozen?" Nashoba asks.

"A few are yeah, but I should still have enough for my back, and maybe even some to sort my face out." Arella looks down at her reflection in the water. "I look awful." She says, quickly looking away. Arella always hates seeing herself looking like this. She'd much rather she was her usual flawless self.

"I'm sure under the purple you look lovely." Nashoba tries to comfort her, but his words don't quite have the right effect. Arella simply carries on mashing berries.

"What's going on over here then?" Nootau says as he walks towards Arella and Nashoba, Mato hot on his heels. "Something smells nice.

"We're crushing barrow berries." Nashoba says.

"Doing what?" Mato questions. Nashoba proceeds to tell them how Arella knows about barrow berries having healing properties, and how she plans to use them to make herself better.

"Interesting." Nootau says. "I've been interested in medicine for a while now. Ujarak's been teaching me bits about it."

"Oh yeah I forgot about that." Nashoba says, the thought clearly slipping his mind.

"He never said anything about barrow berries though."

"I found it out from watching the animals in the forest." Arella admits. "I've seen birds use them, and deer ear them when they have a cough or cold. It worked for that, so it must have worked on surface wounds. I tried it once, on a small cut on my leg. It helped it heal very quickly, and within a few hours, the cut was barely visible."

Arella then proceeded to tell Mato and Nootau about the time she used the barrow berries to heal a poison wound on her face caused by Wolf. Maska enters the clearing at the end of the story, holding four fat rabbits in his jaws. "And there is my warrior." Arella says, pointing at Maska. His chest bristles with pride as she says this. "Brought the berries to me to help me survive, even though he was badly hurt himself. Without you Maska, I would be dead by now." If he could blush underneath his fur, Maska would be bright red.

"But without you, Maska would be dead too right Arella?" Nashoba asks.

"Well that's true." Arella admits. "We owe each other our lives."

"How do you mean he's be dead without you?" Nootau asks. He didn't hear Arella telling Nashoba about this the other day.

"I'll tell you what Nootau." She says. "How about I tell you that story while you help me with my back. Deal?"

"Deal."

Arella feels a little uncomfortable about taking her top off around all these men, but luckily the wound is low enough that she does not have to take it off completely. Nootau moves to sit behind her, while the others stay in front and talk. Maska has dropped the rabbits at Arella's feet and is purring loudly next to her. With her back exposed to the cool afternoon air, Arella tells the story of how she found Maska. Nashoba is hearing this for the second time, but seems just an enthralled as the first time he heard it.

While she is talking, Nootau cleans the wound on her back. The dressing needs changing, and it had gotten dirty again. There is pain while he is doing this, but the questions they all ask about Maska and his mother are helping keep Arella's mind busy.

"So what made you take him on then? Knowing that it was a danger to yourself and that he was an extra mouth to feed?" Mato asks.

"Well I couldn't just leave him there." Arella explains. "Especially after I'd just killed his mother."

"You didn't have a choice though did you?" Nashoba presses.

"Well no, but that's not the point." Arella says. "It was in part my fault Maska's mother died, so it was then my job to look after him." She pauses as Nootau applies the berries to her wound, pain hot on her back. "Plus, if the spirits led her to me, then me to her and Maska, they must have intended this." Arella looks down at the sleeping auron cat next to her. "And I'm glad I have him now." Mato looks like he wants to ask a question, but looks a little uncomfortable about it. "What is it Mato?" Arella asks.

"I was just wondering..." He pauses.

"Go on."

"How did you find it in you to kill the auron cat? Was it hard?" He cringes at his own question.

"You have to understand that I had no choice. She was doing to die eventually, and she asked me to kill her."

"She asked you how?" Nootau says from behind her, breaking his concentration.

"It's hard to explain." Arella says.

"Please try." Nashoba pushes.

"Well, in short, she came to me. I reached out for her, and the auron cat, Maska's mother, came willingly to my hand. When she pressed her face into my palm I saw something. I saw the future, and it was beautiful. I saw myself but older, and Maska how he is now. I knew then that he was meant for me, and that I was to end his mother's life." Arella sighs. "I won't say it was easy because it wasn't, but it was necessary."

By the time Arella has finished telling the story about how Maska came to her, Nootau has finished with the berries on her back. The berries have started to cool the heat, and the redness around the edges of the wound have started receding. Nootau notices this as he finishes up cleaning the excess berries from Arella's back. "Wow. It's working quickly." He notes.

"Told you it would." Arella replies. "The berries are amazing. I don't know of anything they can't heal."

"I'd like to test it someday." Nootau says.

"As long as you're not testing it on me, that's fine." Arella laughs. It's strange having people around her that actually like her, that don't want to get rid of her, or shoe her away. She has a fuzzy warm feeling inside, surrounded by what she can only call her friends. A lump forms in Arella's throat, and she has to make an excuse to get up before tears begin to form. "I'm just going to go have a quick wash in the lake round the corner." Arella says. The men all look around at eachother, unsure what to do. "It would be a great help to me if you could skin and gut the rabbits Maska brought home."

"We can do that." Nashoba says. "Can't we boys?" The others chorus that they can. Arella smiles and turns away from the men, picking up her cloak and fresh clothes as she leaves the stones where they were sitting.

"Maska, you're coming with me too." She calls to the auron cat. "You need a bath and a brush!" Maska gets up from his spot on the ground and follows Arella to the water. They round the corner and keep walking. Arella walks as far as she thinks she needs to in order to be out of sight, then stops. She takes her boots off, unties her hair, removes her clothes and walks into the water, letting it come up to her belly button, but careful for to get her wound wet. She relaxes with the water around her, washing away all her troubles and worries.

When she gets out of the water, Maska is waiting for her. In his mouth is a bunch of barrow berries. "Maska, where did you find them?" She asks, surprised that he found more here. "What are they for?" Maska brings his paw up to his face and brushes it. "For my face?" Arella asks. Maska nods. "Thank you."

Arella applies the berries to her face, then turns to the water. She is still naked, letting her body dry in the air, but her eyes are only focused on her face. Before her very eyes, under the purple of the berry juices, the deep purple and reds of her bruises vanish. After a few minutes of having the crushed berries on her face, Arella washes them off, revealing the marble white skin beneath, now no longer bruised, cut and horrible. Arella has her beautiful face back. She smiles at herself. "Now that's more like it." She turns to Maska. "Now get in the water and have a bath you!" She scolds Maska for not being in the lake already.

While Maska is bathing in the lake, Arella gets herself dressed into fresh clothes. "It feels good to be clean again."

Once she is dressed, Arella begins brushing her hair with the comb she made from a rats ribcage. Sounds disgusting, but the bones are small enough to do the job, and the bones were cleans thoroughly before she used them. She pulls her long hair to the left of her face and begins plaiting it. The plait comes down below her bust, and she ties it with a leather band. She pulls on the plait, loosening it then pulls a few stray strands to the right of her face, letting them frame her delicate skin. She looks in the water, checking everything is balanced, then turns to Maska who has just gotten out of the water. He shakes his great bulk of a body, his long fur now a deeper black, the purple no longer visible with the wet. He's careful to shake away from Arella, knowing that splashing her makes her mad. "Come here Maska. I need to brush you." Arella says to him. He pads over to her and sits on the ground at her feet.

Maska's fur is terribly knotty, but it is therapeutic for Arella to brush it. She starts by his head, slowly pulling out the knots and de-tangling the longer bits around his face. She then moves onto his back, his chest, his legs and finally his tail. Arella must have been brushing Maska for hours, because the sun is on its way down by the time she finishes. She never really gets much time to do this, but the bonding this causes between her and the auron cat is immense.

"We should probably go back to the tree Maska, get some food cooked and go to bed." Arella yawns, and Maska yawns in mirror. "I'm exhausted." She gets up from her spot on the floor, her bottttom numb and cold, and with Maska, starts walking back towards the tree she still calls home.

Arella starts thinking as she walks. "Do you think they genuinely care about us Maska? Or do you think they are helping us for another reason?" Maska just rolls his eyes and stares blankly at Arella. "Am I being paranoid again?"

"Yes you are." Nashoba's voice sounds. Arella jumps. Has she always been this jumpy, or is it a new thing? Arella can't remember.

"What are you doing here? Following me again?" She quips. He caught her off guard, but Arella quickly regained her mental balance. "You're making a habit of that."

"You were gone for a while. We wanted to make sure nothing had happened to you while you were gone." He answers.

"We?" Arella asks, peeking around Nashoba's shoulders to see no one else standing with him.

"Mato and Nootau stayed back at the tree, they're cooking some of the rabbits." Maska looks shocked. Arella looks down at him and rolls her eyes.

"Maska wants to know if you saved one or two of the rabbits raw for him." She says to Nashoba. He thinks for a moment.

"Yeah I'm sure we did. There were too many to fit on the fire at once, so there will still be a couple not cooked." Maska instantly relaxes.

"We'd better get back before they put them onto the fire then hadn't we." Arella says. With that the two of them continue to walk back to the tree, joined by Nashoba now. Arella's been so used to it being just her and Maska, and now there are five. She's not quite sure she will ever get used to it, but it sure is nice to have human company. It's not that Arella doesn't enjoy Maska's company, but it is nice to hear someone else's voice talking back to her.

"You're face!" Nootau says as Arella enters the clearing. "What happened to it?" Arella brings her hands up to her cheeks, wondering what Nootau is talking about. Then she remembers.

"Oh!" She laughs. "Maska found more barrow berries while we were washing by the lake. We crushed them and put them on my face. Amazing work they've done." Arella smiles, her pale beauty shining through, a twinkle in her purple eyes, she feels like herself again, almost.

"That really is amazing." Nootau exclaims. "Do you mind if I touch it?" Arella thinks this is strange, but she allows it.

"Go ahead." Nootau moves close to her, his fingers brushing against the smooth white skin where the angry purple bruises used to be. The skin is still tender, and Arella cringes a little.

"Wow." He says as he brushes her skin. Arella spots Nashoba's reaction as Nootau touches her face. If she didn't know any better, she would think there was a hint of jealousy. She pushes this thought away. She's probably just too tired and hungry to think straight. That reminds her.

"The rabbits." She exclaims. "Please tell me you guys didn't put them all on the fire?" She looks at Mato and Nootau, who has now moved away from Arella.

"We've left two off." Mato answers. "Did you want them all cooking?"

"No, thank you. Maska will eat the two you have not cooked." She ruffles the top of Maska's just brushed head. "He prefers his meat still raw." Mato makes a disgusted face. "Trust me, you get used to it." Arella laughs.

By the light of the fire, with darkness closing in, Arella, Maska, Nashoba, Nootau and Mato all settle in for the night. They've eaten their fill of rabbit, and Arella even cooked up some grue bulbs for their tea. As Arella closes her eyes, Maska's warm body pressed up against her back, keeping the cold of the autumn night away, the last thing she sees are the bright green eyes of Nashoba, watching over her, keeping her safe. He watches her over his shoulder, taking first watch of the night. Not that it is really needed. Maska will wake up if someone gets close, he's grown used to doing that, but Nashoba still feels the need to watch. "Good night Arella." He says as she closes her eyes. Arella simply smiles, and lets her dreams take her away.

Chapter 12

Arella awakens to find the others are already up and about. She sits up, stretching, no more pain in her back. She reaches round to the wound on her back, only to find that it has healed, well almost. The skin in still tender, and softer than normal, but healed all the same. She rolls up the furs she was using as bedding and pulls on her cloak. It's quiet outside, too quiet. Arella wonders if the men have fun off and left her, but why would they? And Maska wouldn't leave her. She pushes the thought from her mind, scolding herself for even thinking it. She leaves the ground hut to fine only Nashoba in the clearing. "Where have the others gone?" She asks as she wipes sleep from their eyes.

"Gone hunting." He states. It looks like he's been busy with something, he's a little out of breath.

"What, Maska too?" Arella asks, noticing that her auron cat is not in the area.

"He led them out. I think they've gone after wild boar or something." Nashoba says. Arella looks around, noticing that things look tidier than normal.

"Have you been clearing up?" She asks him.

"We thought it might be nice if we have a clear out." Nashoba pauses. "Well I did. Afterall, it was my sister who caused all of this." Nashoba is looking at the ground. He's clearly very unhappy about what his sister has done to Arella. She doesn't blame him though. There was nothing Nashoba could have done to stop Nova from doing what she did.

"I tell you what." Arella tries to lift his spirits. "We both have a clear up, then while the others are gone, we start training. I don't know about you, but I could really do with a run."

"A run?" Nashoba questions. "But what about your back?"

"It's so much better now." Arella smiles. She turns and lifts her shirt, revealing the fresh pink skin underneath where the bloody gash used to be. "I think there will always be a scar there, but it doesn't hurt anymore." She says. A warm hand touches her back where the wound used to be, making her jump. Nashoba pulls away quickly, and Arella's cheeks go pink again. She looks to change the subject quickly. "So what is it we're doing then?"

"I was clearing up the dead bushes, and then I was going to sort the chicken coop." Nashoba walks over to the coop. "I know we removed the chickens the other day, but I was thinking we could get some more."

"A nice thought, but with it being this close to winter, and us leaving shortly for the mountains, it wouldn't be right to do." Nashoba looks disappointed. "If we get the coop ready though, I can put more chicken in when we return from the mountains, assuming your sister doesn't have me killed when I get back." She's trying to make a joke of things, but maybe it's a bit too soon for that right now. The smile fades from her face with Nashoba's next words. It might take some time for him to let his guard down with her.

"Don't worry about my sister." Nashoba looks angry. "She has no power over the tribe."

Arella's thoughts turn to the long journey ahead of them. "What about your tribe Nashoba?" She asks. "What happens if..." She's broken off, not wanting to finish her sentence.

"What happens if what Arella?" Nashoba pushes her for an answer.

"What if you don't come back from the mountains?" Arella looks sad, thinking about the people she has grown to care about getting hurt upsets her greatly. "You're meant to be chief. Will they be okay without you?"

"Oh Arella." Nashoba walks towards her, a sad smile on his soft face, not quite reaching his eyes. "If it comes to that, of which I am certain it will not, they will manage. Now please, no more negative thoughts. "

"But..."

"Promise me?"

"Okay." She nods. "One more thing."

"Yes?" Nashoba smiles widely now.

"What will happen when we get back from the mountains? Will I be able to live in peace, or will I have to leave mu home?"

"The others in my tribe respect me, and I think, no I know they will accept you too." Nashoba seems confident about this. Arella smiles now too. It's nice to have him around.

With the help of Nashoba, Arella rebuilds the chicken coop Nova destroyed. They gather more vines and wood from the forest nearby, and within no time at all, the coop looks good as new. "I think I did a good job." Nashoba boasts. Arella bumps into him with her shoulder, knocking him off balance a little.

"What do you mean you did well." She laughs. "I think you'll find I did most of the work here." Arella opens her arms up. "Besides, the main structure was mine." The longer Arella spends with these men, the cockier she is becoming. She likes the new person she is turning into, more confident, more herself.

"True. I'll give you that one." Nashoba says, rubbing his arm where Arella bumped him. "You hit hard for a girl."

"For a girl? What's that supposed to mean?" Arella knows exactly what he means. Women are generally weaker than men, and she knows it. Arella thinks it's funny to make him uncomfortable, to make him have to think about his words.

"I just meant… Well I didn't mean you were weak… I just…" Nashoba doesn't quite know what to say. Arella starts laughing.

"I'm Joking Nashoba. I know exactly what you meant." Arella says to him, calming him instantly. "You really need to stop taking me so seriously." Nashoba smiles at her, taking this on board. "Well I don't know about you, but I could do with that run about now." Arella says, breaking conversation again. "You coming with, or staying here to wait for Mato, Nootau and Maska to come back?"

"They'll be gone a while I think. I might as well come with you." Nashoba answers.

"Good." Arella beams. This is that time when she can really show off. Running is what Arella is good at, and she intends to show him what she can do. She is sure Nashoba won't be able to keep up, but it might be fun to watch.

Arella walks over to the treehouse and begins climbing. It feels good to be able to climb into the tree again. She's missed being able to get high up and hide from the world. She removes her cloak and hangs it in the tree, before also removing her long sleeved top for a vest, and her baggy trousers for more fitted ones. These are the best clothes for running Arella has. They stop her getting caught on branches, and keep her cool. She climbs back down the tree and meets Nashoba at the bottom. She catches him looking at her, but ignores it, or tries to. Her blushing gives it away. Arella is becoming aware of herself. She looked at herself properly for the first time in ages yesterday She is beautiful, with her pale skin and silvery white hair. Aside from the bruising she had yesterday, and the new found scar, Arella's skin is flawless. She examined her body in the dark water the night before, her body toned and beautiful, feminine but strong. "Shall we go then?" She asks. Nashoba nods his agreement.

Arella's intention is to run to the black beach and back. It's not too far, but far enough to get her blood moving and her body going again. She starts off at a slow jog, Nashoba by her side. "So what makes you like to run?" He asks her.

"I like the freedom it gives me, and I like the feeling of the wind in my hair." Arella answers. Nashoba asks a few more questions to Arella, before quietening down. Arella keeps the same pace as before, ducking and diving through the close trees, but Nashoba slows a little.

"Can we take a break?" He asks from behind.

"I took you for a warrior Nashoba." Arella says as she stops and turns back to him, a large beautiful grin on her face. "Not a little girl." Nashoba laughs at this, seeing Arella's humour.

Nashoba stands doubled over, trying to catch his breath. "Where did you learn to run so fast for such a long time?"

"That wasn't fast. That was my normal pace." Arella says. "Was it too fast for you?"

"A little bit yeah." Nashoba admits. "But I'm sure I'll get used to it." He takes a couple of deep breaths then straightens up again. "You'd never guess you were nearly killed by a buffalo the other day."

"It didn't nearly kill me. I was fine." Arella plays it cool. "I just had blood pouring out of my back, and a massive hole in me." She starts laughing.

"Has anyone ever told you you're strange?" Nashoba smiles.

"Never no." Arella beams. Although she's sure people would have told her she was strange if she ever had anyone to talk to. "You ready to go again?"

"I think so yeah." Nashoba answers, and the two of them set off running again. Arella drops the pace down a little for Nashoba, and he keeps pace with her better.

By the time they get to the black beach, both Arella and Nashoba are sweating and tired. "Wow its hot!" Arella exclaims. She takes off her boots and starts rolling up her trousers.

"What are you doing?" Nashoba asks.

"Going for a paddle in the water." Arella says, walking towards the shallow part of the lake in front of her. "Trust me, it cools you down quick." Nashoba takes off his boots too, then rolls up his trousers and steps into the water.

"It's freezing." He says, stepping back out again.

"Cools you down nice and quick though."

"You went for a bath in this yesterday?" Nashoba says, shocked that she went into the water naked.

"Well yeah. I've been doing it for years." Arella states. "You get used to the temperature of the water, and it's really soothing on your skin when you're in it." Arella pulls herself from the water and walks back onto the beach.

"I have sand in my toes now." Nashoba says as he sits down. Arella laughs.

"Sand in your toes feels nice." She smiles, sitting down on the grounds and burying her feet into the black sand. "Makes them all soft too.

"So this is the life you lead then." Nashoba looks up at the sky and smiles. "Running through the trees, hunting animals for food and bathing in cold lakes."

"Hey." Arella leans over and taps Nashoba's bare shoulder, his muscle hard under her touch. She thinks she hurt her hand more than his arm, but doesn't let on. "My life is much more than that." But she knows Nashoba is messing with her. She rolls onto her side so she can see him better while they talk. Both resting on the black sand before the run back to the treehouse. "So tell me about your dad then Nashoba. What happened to him?" Nashoba turns away from her and Arella thinks he's going to clam up and not talk. He does the opposite.

"It was while we were away, on our way back from seeing the elders. They were out on a hunt, my father and a few others. They were out by the red rocks, hunting for buffalo when it came for them." Nashoba sits up and looks across the water. "They said they didn't know what it was, giant wings, black as death, and a huge body, like a bird but not a bird. They've never seen anything like it. The beast swooped down, attacking the men my father was with. He tried to defend himself against it, but the bird thing was too big. It caught his chest with its hooked claws, tearing him open." Nashoba brings his hand up to his face. Arella assumes to wipe a tear away. "They say it killed him right there and then, but I'm not so sure. They all look at me with such pity when they tell me. I think he suffered." Nashoba clears his throat, talking getting difficult.

"That's horrible."

"I found out when we got back to the village. They'd already done the burial ceremony and I didn't even get to say goodbye." Arella feels bad for asking now. Nashoba turns to her, a slight watery glaze over his eyes but smiles. "That's the first time I've told anyone that story."

"Well I'm glad you could tell me." Arella says mirroring his smile. She looks deep into his green eyes. "You know you don't ever have to say goodbye."

"What do you mean by that?"

"Your father is watching over you now, with the spirits." Arella smiles. "All you have to do is talk to him. He'll hear you, no matter where you are. And he's watching over you."

"Thank you." Nashoba says. "I needed to hear that." He clears his throat again, composing himself. "We'd better get back to the treehouse before they do, or they'll be asking questions." Arella and Nashoba both get up from the black sand, dusting themselves off. They both pull their trousers back into place and put their boots back on.

By the time Arella and Nashoba get back to the treehouse, Nootau, Mato and Maska are already back, and they look like they've been back for a while. They've caught a boar, and a decent sized one at that. The boar is already skinned and cooking over an open fire. "Nice catch boys!" Nashoba says to them. They all seem to puff up at this, Maska the most.

"So which one of you caught it then?" Arella asks.

"Nevermind who caught the boar." Nootau winks. "Where have you two been?"

"For a run." Arella says matter of factly. "She knows what they mean, but her and Nashoba genuinely were running. They all stare at them. "No really, we were just running."

"Okay, okay, we believe you." Mato says.

"So who was it that caught the boar then?" Nashoba presses, trying to move conversation on.

"Well Maska found it, then we helped take it down. It was a joint effort really." Nootau says.

"Smells good." Arella breaths in deep, the smell of cooking meat clear in the air. "Making me hungry just thinking about it."

"Me too." Nashoba echoes. He walks over to Mato and Nootau to give them a manly 'well done' hug.

"Gods man, you stink!" Mato cries. "You really have been running haven't you." Nashoba sniffs his own pits.

"Think I might need a bath." He says, looking at the cold lake. "But that water's freezing. Arella looks down at herself. Seeing her sweat soaked clothes, Arella feels she could really do with another bath too, and her clothes need washing. She looks down at Maska, mischief in her eyes. He knows what she is about to be. A twinkle in his eye tells Arella he will follow suit.

They all sit down around the fire, enjoying the cooked boar caught just that day. It's succulent and still pink in the middle, just how Arella likes it. They sit for a little while, but not too long. Days are short, and this one will soon be over.

Once they have all finished eating the boar, and enough time has passed for foo to settle, Arella walks over to the lake, trying to act casual. She walks to the black stones and peers out into the lake. She squints at the water. "What's that?" She says looking down. "Come look." Maska pads over to Arella, and begins staring at the same spot she is. He looks closely, really playing on it.

"You're playing a trick on us." Nashoba says. Not believing her one bit.

"No really, there is something in the water." She leans over for a better look. "It's moving too. I think it might be a big fish." Maska taps the water with his paw. "Don't do that Maska, you'll scare it off." Curiosity gets the better of Nootau and he comes over for a look.

"What is it?" He says as he comes to the water's edge. "I can't see anything."

"There, next to that rocky outcrop." Arella says, pointing to an area of the water.

"Oh I see it now. Yeah looks like a big fish." He agrees, slyly winking at Arella. "Mato come see." Mato comes over, and he too joins in.

"Gods, it's huge." He exclaims, maybe a little too over enthusiastically. "You have to see this Nashoba."

"I don't believe you guys." He says. "There's nothing there." He walks towards them cautiously, still not believing there is anything in the lake.

"Would we lie to you?" Nootau pleads.

"I wouldn't put it past you." Nashoba says. As he comes to the edge of the lake, Arella steps backwards, so does Maska. They leave him standing close to the water. Mato moves behind him. Using all the strength in his arms, Mato picks Nashoba up and with the help of Nootau, the toss him into the lake. He comes up coughing. "Bloody hell it's freezing!" He shouts. Arella kicks off her boots and dive bombs into the water, making a large splash as she breaks the surface. She comes up laughing. "Cold water is good for you Nashoba." She says as she splashes him in the face.

Arella dives down, the crystal clear water is beautiful underneath. So many fish swimming around and bright coloured plants on the bottom. Arella has an evil idea. She swims to the edge of the lake, looking up at the sky above and the edge of the lake. She spots the large frame on Mato above the water, standing dangerously close to the edge. She comes up below him and grabs one of his legs. With all the force she can muster, Arella pulls Mato into the water. He too comes up coughing, complaining of cold but laughing.

"You're not getting me in!" Nootau shouts, turning to run from the water. When he turns, he is met by Maska. He lowers himself close to the ground, breaths in deep and lets out the biggest roar he can. This frightens Nootau, who backs up, his feet close to the edge. Before he has chance to move away, Maska is on him. He lunges for Nootau's chest, catching him off guard and knocking him into the water.

Maska is not the only one not in the water, but Arella doesn't mind this. It was fun knocking everyone into the lake, and at least they're all clean now. After a few minutes of splashing around and swimming, the men start to get out of the water. They are all soaked, and their clothes dripping. Arella swims to the edge of the water, also pulling herself out. "We'd better all get dried off." She says to them. They all move towards the fire, now with the remains of the boar to one side, the fire slowly dying. Nootau pulls another log onto the fire to heat everyone up again. "I have plenty of furs in the treehouse." Arella says. "Maska could you pop up and get them please?" He blinks at her as if to say... *"Why should I?"*. "Do you really want me to climb up there are make the whole house wet?" She asks. Maska reluctantly climbs into the tree and starts nudging down furs. "Everyone grab one, then you can take your clothes off and hang them over there." Arella says, pointing to a low hanging branch. "The furs will keep you warm."

While the others all gather around the fire, wrapped in their furs, Arella takes her furs and gets undressed in the privacy of the ground hut. She kept her back turned while the men changed, and they were grateful for this, although she did peek over her shoulder, catching a glimpse of half-naked men. She decided she wouldn't want to risk them catching sight of her, so she changes in secret.

By the time she is changed, the sun is on its way down. The sky is starting to turn orange, and the men are getting sleepy. It's been a long day, and tomorrow will be even longer. They're going to be practicing fighting and shooting skills tomorrow. Then, if Arella is feeling up to it, set out for the mountains.

Arella sits by the lake, looking out over the water reflecting the bright sky above. A figure joins her, sitting close by. Arella does not turn to see who it is, she doesn't need to. The sweet smell of his skin letting her know Nashoba is close. "Beautiful isn't it." Arella says to him.
"Yes it is." Nashoba says. Arella turns to look at him, and finds him staring into her eyes.

"Are you scared about going to the mountains?" Arella asks him, staring into his bright green eyes.

"A little I'll admit." Nashoba says. "But I trust Nootau and Mato to keep us safe. And I'm sure Maska won't let anything happen to us."

"I guess you're right." Butterflies fill Arella's stomach. She is nervous, and it's not about the mountains. Having Nashoba this close to her makes her stomach dance, her palms sweat and makes her feel a little sick. She looks over her shoulder. "Are the others asleep already?"

"They we're tired." Nashoba says. "Best to let them sleep I think."

"We all need our rest." Arella laughs. Nashoba laughs too, but it's a nervous kind of laugh. They both catch each other's eyes as they look up. Silence fills the air, only broken by the gentle lapping of water at the edge of the lake. Arella looks away, her cheeks flushing pink. Nashoba takes her chin with a shaking hand and lifts it up. He looks at her face, brushing his hand from her temple down her cheek. Arella closes her eyes at his touch, the warmth stopping her shivering. She feels him move in closer, and soon his lips are on hers. A gentle kiss, the taste of him lingering on her mouth, the warmth still burning there even after he pulls away. He stutters, a little embarrassed.

"W...We should probably be sleeping now." He says.

"Y...Yes. Big day tomorrow." Arella stutters. The butterflies in her stomach threatening to take off. Nashoba gets up and leaves Arella sitting by the lake, one last look behind him at the White Ghost wrapped in furs sitting on the black rocks by the lake, bathed in the orange light of the sunset.

"WOW!" Arella couldn't sleep even if she wanted to. Her mind is spinning with excitement She feels dizzy and sick, but she likes it. He likes her. Nashoba genuinely likes her. She could scream she is so happy, but Arella must compose herself. She has to get her rest before they start on their training and gathering tomorrow morning.

Chapter 13

The next day, among the fighting, the dagger throwing, the bow practice and the general preparations, Arella and Nashoba exchanged nervous and embarrassed glances. Neither of them are quite sure how to take the kiss last night, Although Arella can still feel the pressure of his lips on hers, taste the taste of his lips and smell him when she thinks about it. She's never been kissed before, but she liked it. However, Arella is a little confused by his reaction this morning. Does he regret kissing her, or is he embarrassed by it. Arella feels a pang of pain in her chest. Rejection. It's a new feeling for Arella. Being rejected by Nashoba is different than the pain of her old tribe shutting her out. It hurts much more to be rejected by someone you care about. Arella feels cold.

Evening comes, and they're all exhausted. Training went well, and it seems like the men's aim is pretty good now with a bow, although none of them can throw a dagger like Arella. They've also taught her a little about hand to hand fighting, although this was towards the end of the day, and most of what Arella did was watch. Although she was very distracted, Arella thinks she picked up enough to keep her going. It took her right back to four years ago when she first saw the men fighting in the clearing.

They all sit by the camp-site, enjoying the last of the meat from the boar and roasted grue bulbs. "There are a few things we'll need before we can leave tomorrow." Nashoba says, the seasoned traveller in him coming out. "We'll need to make sure the arrows are all sharp, Nootau you can do that. We also need to make sure we have spare clothes; Mato can come with me to our village to get them. And we also need to have food for the journey. I will do that, get some food from the village and bring it back with Mato and the clothes."

"What am I going to do?" Arella asks.

"I don't know." Nashoba says. He'd not thought of anything for Arella to do.

"How about I come to the village with you to get the clothes and things? I can stay in the trees and wait for you to come out."

"I guess that would work." Nashoba says. Arella is a little disappointed that Nashoba doesn't think enough of her to give her a job to do, but she doesn't show it. Maybe it is because of their kiss last night, or maybe because he is scared of her getting hurt. But she knows she can do as much work as they can, and she intends to prove it.

Arella, Nashoba and Mato all get to the edge of the forest, the village the men live in just in sight. They're all low to the ground, Arella's fur hood high over her head, shielding her from view. "We'll go in, then meet you back here." Nashoba says to Arella. "Whatever you do, don't be seen."

"What about you though?" Arella asks.

"What about us?" Mato questions.

"Well, the others aren't going to be happy about you going in, taking a bunch of clothes and food then just leaving again are they?"

"I guess not." Nashoba says. He's not thought of this. Mato lights up.

"What if we sneak in, get the stuff, then sneak out again?"

"We could try it." Nashoba says. "But what do we do if we get caught?"

"Cross that bridge when we get to it?" Mato replies.

"It's about as good as we've got." Nashoba sighs. Arella thinks for a moment.

"I've got it!" She exclaims, then lowers her voice, remembering where she is. "I hide in a tree close to the edge and keep an eye on you. If I see anyone coming your way, I hoot."

"Hoot?" Nashoba and Mato chorus.

"Yeah, hoot. You know, like an owl." Arella explains. "That way you will know someone is about to find you, and you can move out of the way."

"Sounds like a plan." Nashoba says, impressed that Arella thought of something like that.

"Nashoba." Arella says. "Can we talk?" Nashoba looks uneasy.

"You walk ahead Mato, We'll catch up." He says. Mato raises an eyebrow, pulling the scar on his face up a little, but he walks on ahead regardless. "What did you want to talk about?"

"Us." Arella says sternly.

"What about us?"

"Last night?" Arella says. "Last night you kissed me. Now you barely talk to me, and you're not letting me do anything. What gives?" A small tear forms in her eye. Nashoba steps forwards, taking hold of her clammy hands.

"I thought you were ignoring me." He says. "And the reason I didn't give you anything to do was because I didn't want you to risk you getting hurt."

"Come on Nashoba." Arella laughs. "I'm hardly going to get hurt. I think I can take care of myself." She feels a little insulted by this. Arella knows she shouldn't, but its hard to not.

"I'm sorry." Nashoba says, looking apologetic. "You're right. I shouldn't be like that with you."

"I forgive you." Arella smiles. They then move to rejoin Mato, neither of them needing to say another word about it.

"What was that about?" Mato asks.

"I was asking if Nashoba could pick up another fur cloak. I think it might be cold in the mountains." Arella is sure Mato doesn't believe her, but she feels on top of the world at the moment.

So as Nashoba and Mato sneak into the village, Arella climbs into the tallest tree she can find. This is risky in its self. The trees around the edge of the forest are losing their leaves quicker than the others, and this means there is more chance of someone spottitting her. Her cloak should help somewhat however, and the colours of the fur will help conceal her.

From high in the tree, Arella can see the whole village. She watches as Nashoba and Mato duck between the tents, avoiding people as they go. She feels a little bad. Arella is causing some people she has only recently met with properly, people she doesn't really know at all, to steal from their own village and put themselves at risk. "This is wrong." Arella thinks. "I shouldn't be making them do this."

Her concentration is broken. Arella looks back to the village, but cannot see Nashoba or Mato. She panics and jumps down out of the tree. "What if someone saw them, what if they've been caught and..." Arella doesn't want to think of what might happen to them if Nova found them. However much Nashoba says his sister is not in charge, she is vicious. As Arella turns to enter the village, a voice catches her off guard.

"What is the White Ghost doing on the edge of the village?" Ujarak says.

"Shh…" Arella whispers. "You know what I'm doing here old man. I know you say Nashoba and Mato a few minutes ago."

"I did, you're right." He laughs.

"Why are you talking to me? Don't you think I'm bad like the others?"

"I believe that everything happens for a reason. You saved the boys from a wolf four years ago, and now it is their turn to save you." Ujarak says.

"What do you mean save me?"

"I have seen your future dear, I saw it in the fires the night you were here, dying on my table." Ujarak looks dark. "There is pain in your future, and death and suffering."

"What can I do to stop it?" Arella is desperate and scared.

"The future is changeable, but I don't know how to change it. Think of it like a river. It runs strong, and finds the easiest ways through the land, but little streams join that river, sometimes changing its course." Arella looks confused.

"What on earth does that mean?" She asks.

"The smallest thing entering your life, could change your entire future." Ujarak says. He turns and leaves Arella standing. "Just be sure not to take the wrong path." He calls as he moves away.

"Boo!" Nashoba shouts, grabbing Arella from behind. She elbows him in the ribs, not knowing it was him, then turns to find him doubled over in pain.

"Oh gods, I'm sorry. I didn't know it was you. You scared me." Arella rushed. "You jerk! What did you do that for?"

"Well it was funny till you attacked me." Nashoba laughs. Arella starts laughing too. She decides not to tell Nashoba and Mato about Ujarak seeing her, it might worry them.

"So did you get everything?" She asks.

"Have faith pale one, we got everything." Mato jokes.

"You're one to talk." Arella quips back. Nashoba laughs at her. "So have we got everything?"

"I think so yeah." Mato says, looking over his shoulder. "We'd better get moving though, before someone sees us.

"Oh look who it is!" Too late. Nova comes out from the village and enters the forest, Doahte at her heels like a puppy. "I might have guessed you'd be back at some point. Here to kill anyone else White Ghost?"

"Back off Nova, this has nothing to do with you." Nashoba argues with his sister. "We're leaving now anyway."

"With our supplies? I don't think so." Doahte shouts from behind Nova.

"So you've got a voice now, hiding behind my sister." Nashoba says, clearly angry at his once friend. "How does it feel, knowing you're my sisters second?" You could cut the tension in the air with a knife It's very awkward, and Arella wishes she wasn't in this situation.

"I was never a second." Doahte comes out from behind Nova. "She always wanted me, really." He looks back at Nova. "Didn't you?"

"Of course I did. It's just my brother trying to stop us being together. You should do something about it." She says.

"Nova, what is wrong with you. And Doahte is hardly going to do anything against me." Nashoba is a little worried. "Doahte, don't listen to her. She's nuts. You're my friend, you know you are." Doahte is confused. He doesn't know what to do. Arella thinks fast, they must leave now, before the other villagers hear this. She nudges Mato, trying not to make is obvious to Nova that she is planning something. It's not going to be nice, but the only way for them to get away is for Nova and Doahte to not see them get away. She bends to the ground, picking up a stone. Mato spots this. Arella hands Mato one of the stones she picks up, both about the size of her hand. They both move slowly forwards, then together lunge at Nova and Doahte. They take them quickly, both hitting them over the heads, just hard enough to knock them out, not enough to seriously hurt Nova or Doahte. They both drop to the ground, unaware that they were going to be attacked.

"Are they going to be okay?" Nashoba asks, real worry in his voice.

"They'll be fine." Arella says, although she is not so sure, she hopes they haven't left any lasting damage. "They will be fine, and they will wake up soon. They'll only be out enough time for us to get away." She hopes her voice sounds sincere enough to convince Nashoba that they will be okay.

"Okay, let's go then." Nashoba says. With one last look at his sister and the man he used to call friend, Nashoba leaves his village behind, at least for a little while. His life holds more than just living in the village, abiding by the rules set by the elders. He knows this now. He knows life has more to hold than what he has seen so far. Arella has opened his eyes to the truth about the world he lives in.

Nashoba watches Arella from behind as she walks, trailing at the back. Mato is walking next to Arella. They're laughing about something, but he's not sure what. Nashoba missed the beginning of the conversation, lost in his own thought. Arella's hair jumps up and down as she laughs, a sweet laugh, high and bubbly. He loves hearing her laugh, such a happy sound. Arella turns to look at Nashoba, a huge smile on her face. He smiles back at her. That smile could melt his heart a million times over. Is she really worth risking his life, and that of the men he calls his brothers? Of course she is. Nashoba knows now, looking at Arella laughing and joking with Mato, that he would do anything for her. He thinks back to the kiss the night before. Does she feel the same way about him? There's only one way to find that out, to ask her himself, but Nashoba would be too nervous about this. His stomach flips and turns at just the thought. She makes him nervous. Nashoba has never felt this way about a girl before.

Back at the treehouse, Nootau and Maska are waiting. "We were getting worried." Nootau says, his hand on Maska's back. "You've all been gone a long time. We were just about to come looking for you." He looks genuinely worried.

"Well we're back now." Nashoba says. "We just got caught up is all."

"Caught up how?"

"Nova and Doahte, but its okay."

"Are you sure they're not going to follow us or anything?"

"We're good Nootau. Mato and Arella knocked them out. They'll be fine, but we need to get moving before they wake up and follow us. They know where we are, and if we don't leave soon, they'll be able to follow our trail."

"Are they good trackers?" Arella asks, a little worried about them following her and the men to the mountains and running everything.

"Not at all no, but they can follow a little." Nashoba says. "Either way, we should get moving soon. Have we got everything?"

"I just need to get the furs together and wrap them up." Arella says.

"Already done." Nootau adds before Arella can move from the group. He holds up the doeskin back with a couple of the furs tied to it, the others rolled and tied up.

"Well, that saves us a job. Can you carry the furs?" Nashoba asks. He's taking charge of the situation, but that's his job. He is going to be chief one day after all. "Mato you can carry the food. Is that okay?" Then he turns to Arella. "Make sure you always have your bow at hand. I've seen you shoot, and we might need that out there." Then he moves onto himself. "I'll carry the spare clothes and anything else we take. Does that sound okay to everyone?" They all agree with this, not really thinking of anything else they need to do or take with them.

"I just have to get a few things." Arella says, moving towards the ground hut. She picks up her grathon and makes sure her dagger is secure in her boot, then picks up her flint. "Okay, ready."

"Let's go then." Nashoba says. Arella takes one last look at the place she's called home for the last four years.

"I hope I can come back here one day." She says out loud. Nashoba, Nootau, Mato and Maska have already started walking. She turns to catch up with them and finds Nashoba standing behind her. He has a smile on his face, a little sad. "I believe this is yours." He's holding up the red wolf necklace. Arella feels at her chest where the wolf once sat.

"I lost that when the buffalo attacked me." She says, not taking the wolf yet.

"I took it from you." That sad smile again. "It belonged to my mother. My father gave it to her when she was pregnant with me."

"Nashoba I can't take it now knowing that. I just found it in a clearing in the forest. If I'd have known it was your mothers I'd have never taken it."

"I want you to have it. The red wolf if yours now." He holds it out further. "Please take it."

"Will you put it on me?" Arella asks. Her heart beating fast, He nods. Arella turns around and lifts her hair. She feels Nashoba's warm hands around her neck as he tied the leather strap. She turns back to look at him, a small tear on his cheek. Arella reaches up with her hand and wipes the tear away. "Don't cry little wolf, I'll look aftfter it. Promise. " Nashoba smiles.

"I know you will." With that they both look to the forest where the others entered and follow. Neither saying a word to the other, but both knowing the other is right there beside them.

Chapter 14

A light drizzle has started to fall through the sky. Arella pulls her hood up over her head, and so do the others. The raindrops patttter softly on the autumn leaves on the ground, the smell of the forest becoming stronger and more musky in the noses of the travelers. Maska shakes his head, droplets of water flicking from the ends of his whiskers. The rain is not enough to cause them any trouble when walking, but it might make starting a fire tonight difficult. They might have to go without tonight. Arella leads the way for now. They have to go past the area of the forest where she came up against Wolf, Fox, Bison and Goat, deeper into the forest before coming to the mountains. She knows the way to get there, and knows the safest route to the red lands. That's where they will make camp tonight, or that's where they're aiming for anyway. They've been walking for a couple of hours, and conversation has died. The men are nervous about what they might find, and with good reason. Although rumors of the mountain spirits have been told to them since they were young, there is no proof that they even exist. They might get to the mountain and find nothing there. That would be the worst thing that could happen. They would have risked their lives for nothing, and gone all the way to the mountains for no reason. There are also rumors of dark creatures in the forest between the red lands and the mountains. "I've been to those forests before though, and I didn't see anything like the monsters in your stories." Arella says.

"You didn't go very deep in though did you Arella?" Nootau says.

"I guess not."

Arella watches the animals around her closely for signs of danger. She's learned to listen to them and their instincts. With the birds around her chirping happily, Arella has no fear. She also has Maska. He patrols in front of the ground, also knowing the way. Arella trusts him with her life, and he knows this. He keeps an eye on those behind him, making sure they are all safe. Although he isn't really that bothered about the men following behind, Maska will protect them just as he would Arella. She is his everything, and for some strange reason, she cares for the men. They mean something to her, so Maska will protect them. He doesn't understand humans, they're confusing and seem to hurt each other for no real reason. He shakes his head, looking at the trees ahead of him. Maska sniffs the air, the scent of the red lands faint on the air. They'll be there soon, then they can stop for the night.

Arella holds the red wolf in her hand as she walks. It feels warm, like it's alive. She smiles, knowing Nashoba gave it to her. One day she will ask him about his mother, and what happened to her.

But now is not the right time. He's already told her about his father, a story she will never forget. She doesn't want to push him too far too fast.

The trees are growing thinner, and the red rocks have started creeping into the forest. The rain has now all but stopped. Arella lowers her hood again, no need for it here. No one will see her, and the rain cannot make her hair wet anymore. The sun is still hiding behind the clouds, so there is no glare to make her blind. A gruff bird call catches her attention. She turns to see a lone bird sitti-tting on the branch of an old oak tree. His onyx black feather the same as the one in her hair. His white chest and wing feathers contrast the black beautifully. Arella looks around for his mate. "Good morning Mr Magpie." She says, saluting the bird. He caws at her, then flaps his wings and flies off, leaving a black feather to float down to the ground at Arella's feet. She bends to pick it up, placing it in her braid. She looks behind her, the silence unnerving.

"What was that about?" Nootau asks, the other just stare wide eyed at her. Maska rolls his eyes.

"I saw that Maska." She says, then turns back to Nootau. "Don't you say good morning to magpie's when you see them on their own?" She asks.

"No. Why would I say good morning to a bird?" Nootau asks.

"Don't you know the stories?" Arella asks, surprised they don't know this either. "There's a rhyme about magpies." Arella recites an old poem Nayleen used to say to her.

'One for sorrow,

Two for joy,

Three for a girl,

Four for a boy,

Five for silver,

Six for gold,

Seven for a secret never to be told,

Eight for a wish,

Nine for a kiss

Ten for a bird you must not miss.'

"You see, magpies only ever have one mate So if you see one on his own, he must have lost her. If you say hello to him, he won't be lonely anymore." Nashoba, Nootau and Mato stare at her.

"That's madness." They laugh.

"Maybe, but it's something I've always done, and I don't plan on changing my ways." Arella skips on forwards, the new black and white feather in her hair fluttering as she does so.

"She's very strange isn't she?" Nootau says. "I mean I like her, she's different, but strange"

"That she is." Nashoba agrees. "Very different." They all continue on walking, the sky getting brighter again without the clouds.

With red rocks underfoot, Arella knows they must find somewhere to camp soon. Night will fall on them shortly, and if they leave the trees behind completely, they will be in the open for the night with no wood for a fire. "We make camp here tonight." She says, turning back to look at the men. They all look tired, "I thought you were used to walking?" She asks. "Didn't you walk for like four years when you visited your elders?"

"We didn't walk this fast." Mato says. Arella laughs at this.

"I guess I'm used to walking at Maska's pace. Please next time, let me know if we're walking too fast for you." This sounds a little patronizing, and the men do not like it. Nashoba is the only one who doesn't look tired. He's clearly fitter than the others. Arella picks on him to help her build a fire. "Nashoba, can you help me collect wood for the fire?"

"Sure." He says. A cold wind blows over the red lands causing the group to shiver. Winter is well on its way. Arella finds herself thinking that this was probably the worst time for them to be traveling to the mountains. *"I guess it couldn't be helped. Let's just hope we can get to the mountains before the snow hits."*

Arella is busy gathering wood for the fire, Nashoba doing the same while the others sit on rocks close to the edge of the tree line. They look out over the red lands. They've never seen a land this colour. It's different to the plains they're used to, a much deeper colour. Tufts of dead grass grow in clumps, but the red rocks look like they stretch on forever. The lake at the side giving some life, and some grass, but most of this land is dead. "I'm not sure I like this place." Nootau says. "It's so dead"

"Not as dead as you might think." Arella says, overhearing the conversation as she brings back the twigs she's been collecting, Nashoba not far behind her. "There's a lot more life here than it looks like. Just wait for nighttime, then you'll see." Nashoba is already building up the fire. Arella takes the bloodglass dagger from her boot and cuts some of the dead grass from a nearby tuft. She hands it to Nashoba so he can use it to light the fire. "Might be worth waiting till the sun is going down though Nashoba, we need it to keep us warm all night without having to go out and get more wood."

"I'll go get more now." Nootau says. "That way we have space in case it starts to go out in the night." He gets up from the rock her was sitting on, dusts the red off his backside then enters the edge of the forest again, always staying in eyesight of their makeshift camp.

"Maska, will you go with him, make sure he stays safe?" Arella asks. The auron cat gets up from his seated position on the ground and follows Nootau into the forest. With the company of the great cat, Nootau ventured further into the forest, collecting more branches than they would need for this night.

"What should I be doing?" Mato asks.

"Do you know how to fish?" Arella asks him. The blank expression on his face tells Arella he has no idea. "I'll teach you." Arella takes her grathon in hand.

"So that's what that thing is for." Nashoba says. It's clearly confused them all, the bloodglass grathon.

"Well not exactly. It's a weapon, although I've never used it at that. But it works well for catching fish." Arella walks over to the lake and takes her boots off. Rolling her trousers up to her knees she steps into the lake. She lifts the grathon high in the air and stands in silence for a minute or two. Nashoba is about to ask her what she is doing when she brings the grathon down hard, splashing water all over the place. When she brings it out again, a fat fish is caught, wriggling on the end of the sharp weapon. "And that's how it's done."

"Wow. So how many of those do we need to catch to eat tonight?" Mato asks.

"How much food did you bring with you?" Arella asks.

"Not much. We couldn't get more than a sack of roasted grue bulbs before we would have gotten caught." Nashoba answers.

"In that case, we will need another three big fist. One more for us to share, and two for Maska. He can catch his own food, but if he's looking after Nootau, he won't be hunting. Least we can do is feed him." Arella steps out of the lake and hands the grathon to Mato.

"Where are you going?" Nashoba asks.

"Just going to watch from here." She says, sitting herself down on a red rock. "I want you to learn how to do it yourself." Mato takes off his boots and steps into the water.

"It's freezing!"

"And I think it'll be funny to watch." She laughs.

Maska comes out of the tree line, Nootau hot on his heels, arms full of branches. "Do you think this will be enough to last us the night?" Then he sees Mato in the lake, Arella's grathon in his hand, his shirt wet, shouting at the water.

"You stupid bloody fish!" He shouts. "Why won't you just come here so I can catch you?" Arella and Nashoba are doubled over in laughter. "Don't laugh!" Mato looks genuinely angry. "It's a lot harder than it looks." He turns to look at them, water dripping from his face, down his scar and along the lines of his very unhappy face. This makes Arella and Nashoba laugh even more. Mato storms out of the water, causing splashes as he goes. "If you think you can do better, go ahead!" He shouts, the anger clear on his face. It won't last for long, not once Arella gets some food into him.

"I will." Arella boasts, tears in her eyes, sides hurting from laughing so much. She knew asking Mato to catch fish would be funny, but he will learn eventually. They all will. She takes the grathon from Mato, and within minutes, she has caught another three fat fish. "Can you gut them while I get the fire going?" She asks Mato. This gives him a chance to redeem himself.

"That I can do."

Within no time at all, the fire has roared into life, and the fish are cooking over the flames. Maska is digging into his share further away, and the others are already tucking into the grue blubs. "So, do we know where we're going then?" Arella asks. "I mean I know we're going to the mountains, but I mean, when we get there, do we know where the mountain spirit is meant to be?"

"They say he lives deep in the mountains, but not much more of his is knows than that. He turns the sky green in the night sometimes, and it is said that he can be found at the place where the sky meets the mountains." Nashoba explains. "That's what my mother used to tell me anyway.

"I guess we find it when we get to the mountains then." Arella says. She removes the fish from the fire, flaking the skin of the fish to check if it's cooked. The flesh flakes easily, indicating to Arella the they're cooked. She takes all four of the pieces of fish from the flames and hands them out, placed on abaloa leaves she picked up from the forest. They all dig in, satisfying sounds coming from them as they eat. "Have you not eaten fish before?" Arella asks.

"Not in a long time no." Nashoba says, his mouth full of the white flesh of the fat fish.

"A couple of times, some of the hunters brought fish back, but it didn't happen often." Nootau says.

"I can see why." Mato joins in. "Catching fish is hard." They all laugh at this. It's nice to be like this. Arella has always been used to watching from the outside, but this time, she is the one in the middle of the conversations, the laughter, the friendship.

With full bellies, and beds made from furs, Nashoba, Nootau, Mato and Maska all settle down for the night. The auron cat is asleep in minutes. It never takes him long to get to sleep. Arella is also tucked up in her furs. She stares at the stars above her, watching them move slowly across the blackness above. She's struggling to sleep, again. She rolls over and sees that the men are all asleep, except for Nashoba. "Can't sleep?" He whispers to her.

"I never sleep very well away from home. Sometimes I don't even sleep well in my own bed." Arella admits.

"What helps you sleep?" Nashoba yawns.

"Walking." Arella answers, turning back to look at the stars again. Around them, the lightshow that is the crickets has begun. There are no frogs yet, maybe it's the wrong time of year, but Arella can hear a great owl overhead too.

"So why don't we go for a walk?"

"You should stay in bed, you'll be far too tired in the morning if you walk with me tonight." Arella says.

"Don't go too far then." Nashoba says. "I might join you if I can't sleep myself." He closes his eyes, and before Arella even has her boots on again, he is snoring softly.

As Arella walks through the red lands, the only light to aid her the half moon and the stars, Arella recognizes the area. It's been years since she was here, and before she came to defeat the rogues with the poison arrows. This is the area where Arella found Maska in the den, his mother dying at her knife. She spots the tomb where she buried Maska's mother and walks towards it. She kneels on the ground, the hole where she places the great auron cat that brought her everything is covered with the same heavy red stone she covered it with. The grave has not been disturbed. "Thank you." Arella says, looking at the grave, then turning to the stars. "Thank you for bringing Maska to me, for letting me bring him up, for the protection he's given me." A cold wind blows and Arella gets chills down her spine. She takes this as her answer from the gods, they accept her thanks. "If I could do anything to repay this, tell me, let me know." Another blast of cold wind, blowing dear leaves around. A handful of leave fly towards Arella, then past her. She follows the direction they fly in, towards the men and Maska at the camp. "I will keep them safe. I promise. I would lay my own life down on the line to protect them." With this the air goes silent once again.

        Arella goes back to the camp. The fire has started to die, and she can see the men start to shiver in their sleep. They'll wake up soon if she doesn't get the fire going again. She pulls a few of the larger branches, being sure to leave some for the morning, and places them on the fire. It roars back into life, then dies down to a crackle. The heat that comes off it instantly lifts the temperature in the air to comfortable. Arella removes her boots and climbs back into her furs, pulling them tight around her face to keep out the cold. She is soon asleep, drifting into a peaceful dream.

Chapter 15

The next morning, Arella wakes with the light of the sun peeking over the horizon. She looks over to fins Nashoba and Nootau already up, Mato snoring like a bear in his furs still, and Maska yawning, stretching, clearly just woken up himself. Without even putting her boots on, Arella gets up from her furs and joins then men who are awake. They're hunched over something on the red stone floor. "What you looking at?" Arella asks. She wiggles her bare toes, liking the feeling of the rough stones on the bottom of her feet. The ground is still cold from the night, and the chill nips a little.

"We're planning our route." Nashoba says. Arella looks over him and sees a series of lines on the ground. She comes to kneel next to them. "We're here now." Nashoba says, pointing at an area. He circles it with a sick. "We have to follow the lake around to the forest." He draws more lines leading towards the trees he's drawn on the ground. "Once in the forest, the navigation becomes harder." He looks up at Arella. "We'll need your tree climbing skills to look out, make sure we're still heading for the mountains, otherwise we will end up walking off track."

"I can do that." Arella says. "When we get to the foot of the mountain, where do we go?" She asks.

"That I'm not sure. But if we follow the legend, we should go to the top of the mountains, from there we will be shown the way." Nashoba says. Arella is a little skeptical about this, but what does she have to lose.

"I'm going to start packing everything up then, we'd better get moving if you want to get to the forest by nightfall." Arella says. "And I'd like to get some practice in when we get there."

"Practice of what?" Nashoba asks.

"Hand on hand combat." Arella says. "It will come in handy if we come up against another village on the way, or if our weapons are broken. I'm not so good with fighting, not much power behind me, but I'm fast, maybe I can learn to fight." Nootau nods, impressed that she's willing to learn to fight.

"I'll help you pack things up then." The young healer says. They both get up from the red ground, leaving Nashoba pondering over where they go when they reach the mountains. He has slight purple rings under his eyes. He's been up since early morning, trying to figure out where to go next.

Arella and Nootau have to wake Mato up now. A dangerous task by anyone's standards. Normally quite placid, Mato can be more like the bear he's named after when woken from a deep sleep. "He doesn't like being woken up. I've known him to break someone's arm when they woke him in surprise."

"Was that your arm by any chance?" Arella asks, seeing Nootau holding his left arm. She laughs, and so does he. "I have an idea." She walks over to the lake and rustles around in the reed beds.

"What are you looking for?" Nootau asks. Arella comes out of the reeds with a very fat toad in her hand. Nootau starts laughing automatically. "Oh this is going to be funny." Arella walks over to where Mato is sleeping. She moves in close, Nootau and now Nashoba watching. She holds the frog close to Mato's ear and gently squeezes it. The frog croaks, causing Mato to jump. He sits bolt upright, a sharp stone in his hand, aiming directly at Arella. She is too fast for him and jumps backwards, laughter filling the air.

"Wakey, wakey Mato." She laughs.

"What on earth did you just put in my ear?" Mato is mad. Once he sees the frog still in Arella's hands, he sees the funny side of the prank. Maska walks over to him, licking his on the cheek with a rough tongue and fishy breath. "Eww, that's gross!" He says, wiping the catty saliva from his face. "I get it, I'm up now."

With everyone up, and all of their gear packed away, the White Ghost, the Red Wolf, the Young Healer, the Bear and the auron cat all start walking again, following the edge of the lake around, all keeping an eye on the forest in the distance. It's quite a walk away, and with the days getting shorter and shorter, they will have to get a move on to get to the trees in time.

With the ground hard underfoot, walking is fast. There are no roots of trees to dodge around here, and it is easy to see their goal. When they were in the forest, they had to follow the paths made by other animals. These were not always the most direct routes. Looking back from where they have come, Arella can see that the lake dips in and swerves a lot. This would be why it felt like it was taking longer than it should have been. They followed so the lake was directly next to them the whole way round, meaning they walked further then they needed to. Not that it really matters. There is no time frame for them to get to the mountains. Their only limiting factor is when the snow arrives, but there is already snow in the mountains, so not much they will be able to do about this. Arella has pushed that thought to the back of her mind, not wanting to think about what they will do if they are caught up on the mountains in the middle of winter. If it were up to her, they would not have gone until spring, but events have forced her hand. She has to get to the mountains. The mountain spirit will be able to clear her name, then maybe she can finally live in peace.

Looking to the left, Arella spots a herd of horses. They are grazing on the dying grasses of the red lands. There are what looks to be about twelve of them, a few young ones, possibly fouls from this year. "Look Maska, how beautiful is that?" Arella says to the auron cat walking close to her. She turns to look at the men walking behind her and sees Nashoba with his bow aimed at the nearest mare. She runs to him, placing a hand on his, where the arrow meets the bow. "Don't do it Nashoba."

"Why not, it could be food for tonight." He says. Arella knows this is true, but she has a better use for these horses.

"I have an idea." She says. "Let me try it out. If it doesn't work, you can shoot one for dinner. I'm sure Maska would be more than happy to help you catch one."

"Okay, but what madness are you planning?"

"Just wait here." She says to the men. Arella turns and starts walking slowly towards the herd. "You too Maska." She says as she hears the auron cat following behind her. "I need to do this without you boy."

Arella was wearing her cloak with her hood up. As she walks away from the men she unties it, dropping it to the floor. She also drops her grathon here, and takes the dagger from her boot. Arella drops this with the cloak and grathon, now completely unarmed. She walks towards the herd of horses, all of them staring at her. The stallion, a big grey horse, wide chested and a long black mane, white spots on his back, comes out from the center of the herd. He comes out to meet Arella on the red ground. He huffs, pushing hot air out of his nose. Arella lowers her eyes, not looking directly at the horse. He is challenging her, and she does not want to annoy him. It is similar to what she did with the wolves, although not exactly the same. She's never really dealt with horses herself, only seen of them what the men in her tribe did. Although they beat their horses to make them do what they wanted them to do.

The horse taps one front foot on the ground. Arella peeks behind herself, keeping low to the ground. She spots Nashoba with his bow held high again, ready to shoot if the horse attacks Arella. "Lower your bow Nashoba." Arella says.

"But what if it attacks you?" Nashoba says, not moving his eyes from the stallion.

"Trust me Nashoba, I know what I'm doing." This is a lie, but he believes it enough to lower his weapon. Arella really hopes she knows what she's doing. The stallion automatically relaxes, now not under threat from a ranged weapon. Arella peeks through the white hair covering her face, looking up at the stallion. His big brown eyes watch her through long black eyelashes.

Arella moves forwards again, slow and steady. She can tell the stallion is unnerved by her. She doesn't want to make any sudden movements and frighten them. One of the young colts comes to the edge of the herd. He whinny's at Arella. The stallion neighs at him, a warning to stay away. Arella nods at the colt, who then backs off. The stallion needs to accept her in, not matter what the other horses think, if he doesn't accept her, she has no chance with the rest. She extends a hand to the male. He looks at it, staring for a while, before he sniffs at her. He then walks around her. Arella can't help thinking of the similarities with this stallion and the alpha wolf the other day.

Eventually the stallion walks away from Arella. He turns his back on her, accepting her into the herd. Arella enters the center of the herd. The young colt that whinnied at her comes close. Arella extends a hand to him, his coat soft and brown, still with his baby fluff. He presses his face against her hand, enjoying her touch.

"Has she always been this good with animals?" Mato asks?

"Well, she was this good with the wolves yeah." Nashoba says. "I wonder if she's this good with all animals. Might help us in the mountains is we come up against something there. That would make sense I guess."

"What do you mean?"

"Well look at Maska" Nashoba says. "I don't think just anyone would have been able to raise him like that."

"What do you think she wants to do with them anyway?" Nootau asks. If we're not going to eat them, what are we going to do with them." Arella turns back to them.

"We're going to ride them." She says.

"Ride them?" How are we going to ride them without any training or anything?" Nashoba says, unsure of how this will work. "And they're wild horses anyway.

"Not exactly." Arella says. "Remember I said I came from another tribe, and that this tribe all got killed by a passing raiding party?"

"Yeah, so what?" Nashoba says.

"Well some of these horse belonged to my tribe." She smiles. The men have now come closer to Arella, although Maska is keeping his distance. "The four mares over there." Arella says, pointiting to four beautiful looking horses. Two of which are grey, one if deep brown and the fourth is white with brown patches. "They all belonged to the tribe I lived with, and we will be able to ride them." She says.

"I've never ridden a horse." Nashoba says. The others look worried too, and say that they haven't ridden either.

"Neither have I." Arella admits. "But it can't be that hard can it?" She says. Arella has no idea how hard it will be to ride a horse. But they might be able to take them to the mountains quicker. This is her hope anyway.

She moves into the herd, Nashoba, Nootau and Mato staying at the edge. She moves towards one of the mares, wary of her. They're wary of humans, and understandable too. "Nashoba pass me an uncooked grue bulb." She says. He does so, routing around in his bag for one. Arella holds her hand out behind her, waiting for the bulb to land in her palm. When it does, she brings her hand in front, holding the bulb out to the brown and white mare. She sniffs is gingerly, then moves forwards to take a bite. She keeps her eyes on Arella as she bites the bulb, still not sure of her. "Good girl." Arella urges. The mare seems more confident now. The colt who first came to Arella comes over, nuzzling into the mare Arella is attempting to befriend. Looks like she is his mother. The fact that he has come so close to Arella without thinking twice settles her. The mare moves forwards for Arella, lowering her head to a bow. Arella copies this, and the mare seems to accept it. She whinnies at the other mares, and they all step forwards, eager for grue bulbs themselves. "Everyone take a bulb and pick a horse. If you move slow, you can attract them to you. The horse should come to you. If you scare her off, you won't have a horse to ride though. All drop your weapons; they unnerve the horses." The men follow her lead, and soon they have their own horses tamed and willing to let them close. This was much easier than Arella thought it would be. She's beginning to think that the spirits are on her side, trying to help her find out who she truly is.

The men spend the next half hour getting to know their horses They bond with them, getting to know the way the feel, learning how they move when they walk. Nashoba comes over to Arella who is with her brown and white mare, his deep brown girl following him close behind, nibbling at the back of his shirt. "Shouldn't we be moving soon? If we're to get to the forest by nightftfall? " He asks.

"We will go soon." Arella says. "Not as much of a rush if we can ride."

"I guess not." Nashoba says. "How did you know you would be able to tame the horses to be ridden?" He asks.

"I didn't, it was just a hunch, but it worked." Arella admits. "I've learned to follow my instincts and just to go with them. If I feel something, it must be for a reason." With this, Arella feels the hair on the back of her neck stand on end. Something isn't right. She looks around, alert, trying to spot the thing that is making her nervous.

"What is it?" Nashoba asks.

"Shh." Arella urges, trying to listen. The mares are on edge too. Seeing that Arella is worried has spooked them a little. Her mare stays close to the, the rest of the herd not now belonging to them have wandered off a little except for the young colt. They've even now let Maska get close, deeming him no longer a threat. "Something's wrong." Arella whispers. At that moment, a bark sounds, alerting her to the danger. "Hunting dogs!" She shouts. "Quickly, on your horse and go, to the forest."

"Can't we fight them?" Nashoba says, climbing onto the back of his brown mare, Nootau and Mato struggling a little with their. Arella runs to them, giving Nootau a hand up. By the time she gets to Mato, he is already on the grey mares back. Arella turns to look at Nashoba. He can see by the look on her face that she is serious. Arella has heard of the devastation hunting dogs can create, and doesn't want to be their prey.

"No we can't fight them. They're way too fast and I don't have enough arrows for a full pack." The dogs are almost on them. "Quickly go!" Arella shouts. Nootau and Mato are on their way, not needing to be told twice to run. They gallop off, their horses carrying them quickly over the red rocks. The rest of the herd have scattered, but the dogs keep coming. Arella can see them now, their black matttted fur clear on the red rocks, small in size but great in numbers. There must be fifteen of them, all snapping and snarling. "Nashoba go, I'm right behind you!" Arella says.

"I'm not leaving until you are!" He shouts, determination in his voice. Arella smacks the backside of his brown mare hard. She jumps into action, running away from the dogs, Nashoba on her back.

"I said go!" Arella turns to the dogs. They're fast, too fast for Arella to get onto the mare's back now. She gently slaps her mare's backside too, causing her to start running. The colt joins suit, following by its mother's side. The first dog is upon Arella. She dives to the ground, grabbing her cloak, bow, quiver and grathon and swinging it at the dog. She catches it in the face with the shaft, knocking it over. She then picks up her cloak and dagger, shoving it into her boot and pulling the cloak on fast. The dog is on its feet again quickly, but Arella is too fast for it. She is running at full pelt, Maska close by, not leaving her on her own. The dog is hot on Arella's heels, but Maska's got this. He dives on the dog, taking it out instantly. He's faster than Arella is, so will catch up quick. A cry of pain from the dog as Maska crushes its throat pushes her on. The other dogs won't be far behind, and although they are pack hunters, they don't have very good stamina. They will tire soon, but not before Arella. She must get to her horse quickly.

Arella moves as fast as her legs will carry her. She comes up alongside the horse. She knew she was fast, but this is taking it to a new level. She actually just caught up to a horse. She can't think about that now though. The mare looking at her with wide eyes, genuine fear there. Arella spots the colt next to her. This is where her fear is coming from. The mare knows the colt is not fast enough to outrun the dogs. This is the only reason Arella caught up to them, and if she can catch up, the dogs will have no problem. Arella takes a handful of the mare's main and uses it to pull herself up onto her back. This causes the mare no pain, and once Arella is on her back, she settles a little.

The thundering of the horse hooves, mixed with the barking and growling of the hunting dogs is almost deafening. Mixed with the beating of her own heart, Arella is struggling to concentrate.

"Maska, I need you to stay close, keep the dogs off us." Arella says. The auron cat moves in close, keeping one eye behind him, in case the dogs come up close. Arella stand up on the back of the mare, using her balance. This is hard, the mare is moving a lot, and the ground is uneven. Once turned around, Arella sits back down again, this time facing behind. She pulls her bow off her shoulder and knocks an arrow. Aiming directly at the first dog she catches eyes on, Arella pulls the arrow back and fires. She catches the dog in the eye, causing it to fall head first to the ground, rolling a couple of times before stopping dead. She knocks another arrow, aiming at a second dog, and again hits her mark. She's chosen not to use the bloodglass arrows, knowing they won't be able to go back to get them. They just keep coming. A dog comes up close. Maska takes this one out while Arella is getting another arrow ready.

      They're coming up close to the forest now, much quicker than Arella ever intended. The horses will be tired now, but at least they are alive, for now. The dogs start to back off, realizing they will not get this hunt today. Arella lowers her guard a little, and her mare begins to slow. Out of one of the nearby bushes, a dog appears. It jumps at Arella on the mare's back before she can pull an arrow from her quiver. It catches her off guard, knocking her from the back of her horse. The dog, snapping jaws, bits for Arella's face. She holds it off with her hands, but it's strong. A terrible stench escapes the hunting dogs jaws, dripping sticky black saliva onto her face as it tries to bite her. It's skin is hard to hold onto, and Arella's hands keep slipping from the dogs throat. It lunges closer, catching a sharp black tooth on Arella's cheek. She cries out in pain and fear. An arrow suddenly comes from nowhere and lands in its shoulder. The dog backs off from Arella's face a little, the pain clearly making it think twice. Arella has time to reach for her dagger in her boot. The dog comes back for her again. Arella brings her hand up quickly, jabbing the dagger deer into the skull of the dog through it's open jaws. As she pulls the dagger free, a few of the dogs' teeth catch her arm, ripping at the skin as she pulls free. She rolls away, the carcass of the dog lying bleeding on the floor. Arella looks up to see Nashoba with his bow in hand, ready to fire another Arrow if Arella had missed the dog with her dagger. "Thank you." She says.

Chapter 16

Arella has blood on her face, and a dead dog at her side, but she's alive. If it weren't for Nashoba, she herself would be dead. She thanks him again as he steps forwards to help her up. His hand reaches down for her, and Arella takes it gladly. She can feel a deep pain in her shoulder where she hit the ground. "That's going to be a lovely shade of purple in the morning." Arella says, rubbing her shoulder.

"We should get away from the red lands, in case the dogs decide to come back." Nootau says.

"Agreed!" They all chorus.

Arella walks over to the mare she's taken as her own and the colt who clings to his mother. She strokes the mare's nose, calming her. "Shh, its all over now." The mare is breathing deep, the colt too, both wide eyed. "The dogs have gone now and you're safe." Arella then pulls down a vine from a nearby tree, tying it around the horses' muzzle and head, making a makeshift bridle. "We can't ride the horses for a couple of hours, I guess that will take us to night time." Arella says, stroking her horses mane.

"Why not?" Nashoba asks.

"They're tired from running, we should give them a break. They will be okay to ride in the morning though." Arella explains. The others seem to understand this now. "Copy me with the vines, then you can lead your horse." Arella says.

While the men are tying their bridals, Arella washes the blood from her face in a shallow stream. The water runs a deep red as she washes, the metallic smell leaving her. She washes until the water runs clear again and she can no longer smell the blood. *"I'm never going to get used to the smell of blood."*

Once the bridals are all tied, Arella checks to make sure they are not too tight. "Okay, lets get moving then." She says. "There's an old Willow tree in these parts I know will keep the rain off us if it starts." She looks down at Maska. "Can you remember the way there boy?" He looks at her as if to say, "How could I forget." There's nothing to fear from coming over to this side of the lake now, no rogues with poison arrows, but Arella still feels a little uneasy. She pushes this thought away and starts walking, taking lead of the group, with only Maska ahead. She can still smell something metallic. This time it's her own blood. The hunting dogs teeth cut her arm deep and the blood is still flowing slowly fro the cuts. It's started to slow now though and will soon scab over.

The forest on this side of the lake is strange, less deciduous trees and more conifers. As a result of this, this forest is darker, the trees not shedding their leaves, light struggling to get to the forest floor in parts. Arella looks up at what little sky she can see. It is startiting to turn red. "Maska, how far away from the willow are we?" He looks up at her and blinks. She takes this as an indication that they are not far. Within minutes, they can see the willow. It is a welcome sight. They move closer to it, the cover of its leaves calling to them. The air has a bitter bite to it now, and the wind has picked up. "We have to get a fire burning soon." Arella says. "Before the cold sets in."

She sets to work tying the horses up, while the others collect firewood and kindling for the fire. It doesn't take long until they have a fire burning, and the air around them is dark with night. "Do you think we're far enough away from the wild dogs?" Nootau asks, looking around for any sign of them.

"They won't come into the forest." Arella reassures him. "They don't like the trees and grass beneath their feet. Besides, the horses will know if there is any danger around. So too will Maska." She smile. "We can feel safe sleeping tonight."

Arella's stomach starts to growl. "Do we have any food?" She asks. Nashoba roots around in his bag.

"We have some cooked rabbit legs." He pulls them out. "Six of them." He hands them out, one to everyone.

"Do you want to hunt for something Maska, or are you waiting till morning? " Arella asks the great black cat. He simply yawns and closes his eyes, his fluffy head resting on his massive paws. "Morning it is then." She laughs, tucking into her rabbits leg.

"Who gets the last two legs?" Mato asks, finishing his off first.

"I don't mind." Arella says. "I'm not all that hungry." The men decide that Mato should have one of them, seen as though he is the biggest, and Nootau should have the other. They tuck into them greedily.

Arella looks over at the horses. They are huddled together under the edge of the willow tree, heads hanging low, grazing on the moss that covers the ground. She smiles at them, knowing they're safe and that her and the men have horses to help take them to the foot of the mountain at least. It will help them get there much faster. Her shoulder aches, but Arella still doesn't feel tired tonight. Maybe it's the anticipation of what they will find as they venture further into the forest, but she just can't sleep. The others seem tired, and they're soon settling in for the night. The others have all fallen asleep already, leaving Arella to think in the darkness. In her boredom, Arella has started picking at the scabs forming on her arm.

She's thinking back to the first time she saw Nashoba, Nootau, Mato and Doahte. Doahte, she wonder what will happen to him when they get back to Nashoba's village.

Arella sits, staring at the fire, the flames dancing in the dark. She hears a noise, a crack of a branch. She sits bolt upright instantly, her dagger raised in her hand. The blackness around her disorientatiting, the base of the tree at her back. Nowhere to run if danger is in front. Arella's heart is beating fast, fear filling her blood, making her cold. "It's just me." A voice in the darkness. She'd recognize that voice anywhere.

"You scared the living daylights out of me Nashoba." Arella says, her heart now beating fast for a different reason. "Why aren't you sleeping like the others?"

"I saw you awake, and I didn't want you staying up on your own again." He says. "Where did you go yesterday?"

"I just went for a walk." Arella lies.

"Come on Arella, I know your lying voice, and that's exactly it. If I could see your face right now, I'm sure you'd be bright red too." Arella lifts her hand to her cheek. He's right, her face is warm.

"I went for a walk, that much is true. But I found something." She says. Nashoba stays silent, waiting for Arella to carry proceed on her own. "Remember I told you about when I found

Maska's mother near my home, and I followed her to her den. Well I found the tomb I buried her in. I stayed there for a while, then came back. That's all." Arella does not tell Nashoba about the spirits and the wind leading her to them, and she hopes Nashoba doesn't pick this up in her voice.

"Oh." He says. "Well I'm sorry to hear that you found it on your own. You must have been upset."

"A little. But it was four years ago, and I'm happy I got Maska out of it."

Arella smiles in the darkness. Now she is not looking directly at the flames, she can see the forest surrounding her. Things are slowly coming into focus, including Nashoba. He looks beautiful in this light, the flames dancing on his red brown skin, the slight breeze in the air causing the free strands of red brown hair to flow. His green eyes alive with life and hope. She smiles, a smile meant only for him and dares to ask him a question. "So will you tell me about your mother?" She asks. The silence that follows makes Arella think she shouldn't have asked. Maybe she's just pushed him away again. Then he speaks.

"She was an amazing woman, strong and beautiful. Everyone said she was." Arella looks over to him, but finds him looking away. "She was the one who taught me most of what I know. It was when she fell pregnant with Nova that things changed. She stopped spending time with me, got very ill. I thought it was my fault, but Ujarak said it wasn't. My sister was born, and things started getting better again. I was ten when my mother died, Nova still small. We don't really know how it happened, just that she started getting ill again. She got worse, over the course of a few months. It was winter when she passed. I was by her side when she went. Nova doesn't really remember, but I do." He falls silent.

"Thank you." Arella says, placing her hand on his for comfort.

"Why are you thanking me?"

"For opening up and telling me something as personal as that." Nashoba stares at her.

"It feels like I can tell you almost anything." Nashoba says. "I don't know what it is about you, but something is very familiar."

"Maybe it's because I used to stalk you." Arella laughs. "Or you used to stalk me." He then laughs at this too, the mood lifting a little.

They both sit in silence for a little while. Nashoba yawns. "You should go to bed." Arella says.

"Not until you do." He answers back, yawning again.

"Okay." Arella says, laying down on her side. "I'm lying down to sleep now." She pulls the furs up tight around her neck and stares at the fire. She feels Nashoba lay down on the ground close to her. Within no time at all, he is snoring softly again. Arella laughs softly to herself. Nashoba falls asleep way to fast. It's nice to know he's relaxed enough to do so though.

In the light of the next morning, Nashoba is leading the way on his brown mare. He has a better sense of direction than the others. "If we keep walking up, checking with the trees every now and then, we'll be able to go in a straight line." He says as they walk.

"Are you sure you know where you're going?" Nootau asks.

Nashoba sighs. "Arella can you climb into the tree and just check we're going in the right direction?"

"I'll give it a go." She says. Arella's shoulder is still hurting from the day before, but it's not as bad as she thought it would be, and being her left side, it's not affecting her too much. She dismounts her horse and begins climbing a nearby pine tree, moving quickly but safely. From the top of the tree she can see for miles around. "Good job I'm not scared of heights!" Arella calls down. As she looks over the tops of the trees, she spots a brown spider with yellow stripes on her legs weaving a web. She smiles at the beauty of nature before looking to the landscape ahead

The forest stretches on for miles a sea of deep green, broken in places but Arella cannot see what by. Beyond that, the grounds look to slope slowly to the base of the mountains. They cover the horrizon as far as she can see. Beautiful rocky mountains, capped with fresh white snow.

"What do you see?" Nashoba shouts back up.

"We're going in the right direction. It looks to still be about five or six mines to the foot of the mountain. We'll have to see if we can make it there before nightfall." She then starts climbing back down the tree.

"I didn't realise the mountains were that close." Mato says.

"Well, the foot is about there. They go a long way up though before we'd reach the top." Arella says. "As long as we get there by nightfall though, we should be okay." Arella says.

"Why are you so worried about not getting there before the sun goes down?" Nashoba asks.

"I had a dream last night." Arella says. "It wasn't a good dream. All I can remember of it is something following me. It was dark, and I couldn't see what it was, but it made me very uneasy. I have a bad feeling that the thing from my dream is here, in the forest. I want to get out of here as soon as we can." She shivers, the hair on her arms and neck standing on end. " She mounts her mare again and they start walking once more.

The walk through the forest is much quicker with the horses, and Arella's back is hurting a lot less. It was hard going, having to carry everything on her back. She's glad they came across the herd when they did, and that she's seem people tame them before.

Every half an hour or so, Arella has to climb a tree to check that they are going in the right direction. Most of the time they are, but there are a couple of occasions when they have to change direction slightly. The mares and foul seem to be doing pretty well in the forest, and they are making good headway, much better than without them.

A drop of rain falls from the sky, landing in the middle of Arella's head. She looks up into the sky, seeing more and more rain falling through the tree cover. As clouds roll over, and the rain begins to fall, the darkness descends. With the closeness of the trees, the canopy with barely any gaps, what little light the sky was providing is all but gone. Arella has a sinking feeling, and the darkness continues to close in. "We need to get out of here. Fast." Arella says with some urgency.

"I think you're being silly." Nashoba says.

"Yeah, it's just a little rain." Nootau says. Mato is not so sure.

"Guys something doesn't feel right." He says.

"Not you as well." Nashoba says. At that moment, Arella's mare spooks. She rears back on her hind legs. Arella manages to keep her balance and stay on her back. The other horses are starting to spook too, although the men manage to keep them under better control. "Maybe you're right." Nashoba says. "Let's keep moving." He picks up the pace a little, not wanting to be caught in the rain with whatever it is that's spooking the horses.

The rain gets heavier, and the thunder from above begins to sound. Flashes of light brighten the forest floor, but they spook the horses too. The deeper into the forest they walk, the darker it gets. Arella has a very funny feeling about this place. She does not like it at all. As they walk, Arella can feel something, and it's not a nice feeling. Eyes watching her. She can't escape the feeling of being watched. She turns to look behind her and sees them. Two great big red eyes looking at her in the darkness. She kicks her horse into gear. "Move!"

Chapter 17

Arella is frightened. She's not sure what it was she saw behind her. She only remembers its red eyes. Her and the men are fleeing now, their horses carrying them as fast as their legs will take them. Arella looks behind. The red eyes are following her, and the creature to whom they belong is coming closer. In a flash of lightening, Arella gets a glimpse of the beast that peruses them. Its red eyes set in a wolfs head of sorts, although the fur on its head has come away in places, leaving only the red raw flesh beneath. Although its head is that of a wolf, the creature has the horns of a stag, huge and threatening. It charges towards Arella and the group fast, moving on two legs like a man, although it must be nearly seven feet tall. Its arms and legs thin, nothing more than skin on bone, the fur eaten away in places, red raw skin beneath clear to see on the ribs and one arm. It stretches a long arm out, human hands on the end, reaching for prey. Its huge feet on the end of long legs crush branches on the ground, causing devastation as it runs. The horses and panicked now. A strong breeze comes in from the rear, bringing with it the stench of rotting flesh. Arella's horse's eyes widen and she throws her head. She manages to keep control, just.

Arella looks down, Maska at her side. "Run ahead Maska, your faster than the rest of us." She shouts at him, panic in her voice. "Find us a safe route through the forest." Maska runs ahead, looking over his shoulder, checking to make sure Arella is still behind him.

"What is it?" Nashoba shouts. The fear clear in his voice too.

"Don't look back." Arella says. "Just keep your horse moving. If you look back, you'll unbalance your horse." This isn't exactly true, but she doesn't want the men to panic when they see the beast that's perusing them.

The thundering of the horse's hooves on the ground echo in the forest, bouncing off the trunks of the pine trees. Arella's mare is breathing hard, steam coming from her nostrils as she runs. Arella's heart is beating fast. The trees passing in a blur. A branch from a pine scratches her face as she passes a tree, drawing a thin line of blood under her right eye. Watching the backs of the men who flee in front of her, focusing only on them not the beast that follows, they push on. Arella can see Maska ahead, trying to find a safe path for them. He keeps turning back, worry on his face. They duck and dive through the forest, weaving around the trees, not taking a direct route at all. Every time Arella looks back, the beast is closer, and the other horses and further away.

The beast roars, a cross between a deer's roar and a wolfs growl, a hallowing noise. It sounds close. Arella peeks behind again, this time to find the beast much closer. She is at the back of the group, her mare reluctant to leave its colt. Arella tries to push her on further, but the mare is too stubborn. The colt trips on a root on the ground. Arella looks back to see it get up. It's not quite grown into its legs yet, finding them too long and gangly. He struggle to get back to his feet, getting tangles in some loose vines on the ground. The beast is on top of it before it can get its footing on the freshly slick ground. It grabs the colt with a large hand, claws digging into the colt's chest, squeezing, blood dripping from its nails. It's stopped to feed on the colt. Arella's horse slows to a halt. "Come on you silly horse." Arella shouts at the mare, kicking at her kind quarters. "Move or we'll be next." The mare bucks on her hind legs, knocking Arella to the ground. She falls with a thud to the floor into a large puddle. With the wind knocked out of her, Arella is unable to get up. She lays on the wet ground, struggling to catch her breath again. Her mare turns back towards the beast, now feasting on her still living colt. She whinnies loud, charging at the beast It raises its head from its meal and growls, its white teeth shining through the blood dripping from its mouth. Arella feels sick just looking at it, her head swimming. She should be up and running, she should be far away by now, but something is stopping her moving. Her fear is keeping her pinned to the ground.

The mare Arella called her own, having paused at the growl from the beast, now charges full pelt at it. Arella does not know what she intends to do, but whatever it was failed before she even though about moving. The beast lowers its head, leaving its horns pointing in the direction of the mare. Before she can stop, she has impaled herself on the antlers. He screams deafening and horrifying. Arella looks away before the horse hits the antlers, but she cannot escape the sound. Arella covers her ears, and puts her head into the ground, trying to block out the sound of the dying mare with her own screams.

Scratching at the back of her neck, teeth ripping at her shirt. It's got her. Arella starts screaming, her eyes closed tight, not wantiting the beast to kill her. She thrashes her arms around, hitting at the beast that holds her. A hand grabs her arm from above. "That's it." She thinks. "This is the end." She looks up at the beast about to kill her, determined to look it in the eyes before she dies. When she opens her eyes she sees green, not red. Nashoba grips her arm tight, pulling her up with such force. He hauls her up onto the back of his mare, Maska at his side. "Come on, we have to go!" He shouts. The others kept running, so they're a way off. Nashoba kicks the mare into gear and they speed off. Arella looks back at the massacre behind her, the beast busy feeding on the mare and her colt. "I think that might have bought us some time." Nashoba says. Arella can't divert her eyes away from the bloodbath they left behind. If she had anything left in her stomach, she is sure she would have left it on the forest floor.

They rush through the forest, Nashoba and Arella eventually catching up with Mato and Nootau, Maska caught up a few minutes earlier, leading the way to their scent. "What was that?" Nootau says as Nashoba and Arella enter the clearing they've stopped in on one horse.

"I don't want to hang around to find out." Nashoba says. "We should keep moving." He moves his horse onwards in a slow canter, the others following on. Arella sits on the back of Nashoba's horse is silence, holding tight to his waste so not to fall off. Nashoba lets himself drop to the back of the pack. "Arella you're going to squeeze the life out of me." He laughs, if a little nervous. Arella lets go quickly, suddenly realising what she is doing.

"Sorry!" She gasps.

"It's okay." Nashoba says, still nerves in his voice. "Is that the thing you saw in your dream?"

"I... I don't know... I mean, I think so." Arella stutters. "Whatever it was, it'll be back for us if we don't move quickly."

"Agreed." Nashoba says. "This has set us back quite a long way now. He shouts to the men in front. I think we need to find somewhere safe to camp for the night before finding our way to the mountain tomorrow." He sends Maska ahead to scout out somewhere to hide.

Arella is forever looking behind, checking the monster is not chasing them anymore. She cannot hear it, but then the rain is dulling everything around. In between the cracks of thunder and the flashes of light, Arella can see nothing but the forest around her and the men she travels with. Maska comes out from behind a tree, signalling that he's found somewhere for them to camp for the night. Arella dismounts Nashoba's horse and goes to him, her hair dripping set, shivering to the bone. "Okay Maska, what did you find?" He leads Arella around the trees, the passage getting thinner and thinner, surrounded by rock. Arella calls back to the men. "We're going to have to leave the horses here."

"Why, where does it go?" Nashoba shouts back around the corner. He comes up to where Arella is standing. "Whoa." He exclaims. Maska has found a cave. It leads from the forest, through a narrow gully then presumably into the cave. Maska has been inside, but no one else has yet entered.

"Did you check there are no bares or anything in there Maska?" Arella asks. He just looks at her as if to say "Bears, really through that gap?".

"Well you never know Maska, if the cave has a second entrance…" Maska rolls his eyes. "Of course you checked it." Arella turns to look at the men behind her. "We'll have to leave the horses here, they won't fit in the cave, but that means neither will that creature."

"That's true." Nashoba says. "Just a shame we have to leave them behind."

"Yeah, I was getting used to not walking." Nootau laughs. A roar from deep in the forest makes them jump.

"I think we should get inside now." Mato says. He takes his things from the back of his grey mare, and the others follow suit.

The entrance to the cave is very narrow. Maska and Arella pass through rather quickly, Arella being slim and Maska being low down. The top of the cave entrance is narrower than the bottom. It takes a good couple of minutes of walking for them to get through. "Does anyone else feel like we're going down?" Arella asks. She turns to find Mato struggling to get around a narrow corner.

"Can't say I've noticed to be honest." He says, his face pressed up against the wall of the passage, Nashoba and Nootau pushing from behind. Arella takes his free hand and pulls. He comes through the gap, followed by Nootau and Nashoba.

"Maska, are we nearly there?" Arella asks. The auron cat meows and nods his head once, a small gesture, but Arella knows its meaning.

Arella rounds another corner, following Maska. Although the rain outside stopped just as they entered the cave, water still tickles down from the roof through tiny holes. There isn't much light in the passage, and Arella keeps tripping. She trips again, this time over a large stone. When she falls, she lands on the ground. Expecting to be in a confined space when she gets up, Arella is surprised to see that there is space around her. The cave has opened up, and it is now a rather large space. It's also fairly well lit, with light from above streaming in through the gaps in the cave roof. A large tree has spread its roots out underground and broken into the cave. The roots stretch all over the cave, all tangled up in a mess. "You have to see this!" Arella shouts back to the men tagging behind. They enter the cave too, and one by one, their jaws drop.

"This place is amazing." Nootau says. "Is that a real tree?"

"Well what else would it be?" Nashoba says. Equally as amazed as the others.

"First things first." Arella says. "We have to build a fire. I don't know about you, but I'm freezing, and my clothes are wet."

Mato and Nootau set to work collecting dead roots from the tree that has invaded the cave. They pile them up, not a huge pile, but enough to dry them off and stave off cold at least. Arella explores the cave a little more. She walks around the edges, dripping with water, moss growing on most of them. There also looks to be something else growing on the wall. Arella inspects it further. Mushrooms. The same type she has seen growing in the forest near her home. They're edible, but don't taste particularly nice. She picks them all, placing them in her deerskin bag. She continues on around the edge of the cave, picking up more mushrooms as she goes.

At the back of the cave, Arella finds another opening. This looks to lead straight out into the forest again. She peeks out through the hole, big enough for her to pass through, and probably just big enough for Mato, although he might struggle. The sun is now on its way down, and the forest will soon be plunged into total darkness. The orange glow of the sun is making it hard for Arella to see out. "I'll look again in the morning." She says to herself, deciding that through here would probably be safer than going back through the cave to the other side. If the monster followed them, at least it wouldn't be able to track them through the cave system.

"Do we have any food?" Mato asks.

"I have mushrooms." Arella yells back. She then goes to the men who are under the mangled roots of the trees, stoking the fire up.

"Mushrooms? Are they safe to eat?" Nootau says.

"They're the same ones we get back at home. They don't taste so good, but they're edible." Arella says.

"Do we have to cook them?" Nashoba asks.

"You can tell you don't do the cooking back at your village. We don't have to cook them, but they taste a little better cooked." She laughs. "If we thread them onto sticks, we can roast them over the fire. It's not much…" Arella says, placing her arm full of strange grey mushrooms on the floor next to the fire. "But it's something at least."

"What about Maska?" Nashoba says. "He's not eaten in a couple of days now." Nashoba's question is answered by the dying squeal of a rat. "Ah. I guess he can catch his own food." Arella starts laughing.

"Maska normally catches his own food. And he's used to going a few days without food." While the mushrooms cook, Nashoba, Nootau, Mato and Arella all sit around the fire. "I really need to get out of these wet clothes." Arella says. "They're rubbing really bad." She starts to blush. "Erm… Could one of you guys erm… Look away so I can get changed?"

"Maybe I don't want to look away." Nootau winks at Arella. "Joking, I'm joking We'll turn away." He laughs. Arella sees Nashoba shoot him a dirty look out of the corner of her eye.

"Thank you." She says. She waits for the men to turn around before she starts to undress.

Once she is in dry clothes, Arella takes her wet ones and hangs them from the roots of the dead tree. "You can turn back around now, I'm changed." Arella says. She pulls her long white hair round the her front and begins brushing through it with her fingers. Her hair is matted with mud from her fall, and she's lost her magpie feather. She's glad she can't see her own reflection here. She must look a right state.

"I think I might get changed too." Nashoba says. "I'm a bit wet." The others all decide to do the same. Arella turns her back, so not to see them getting changed. She can't help but peek over her shoulder. Luckily for them men, they are all wearing trousers by the time she peeks, but Nashoba's bare chest is in view. Arella turns back quickly, before he notices her looking but she has a sneaking suspicion he caught her looking anyway. That image will be forever etched into her mind. His well sculpted body, beautifully smooth and deep reddish brown. Arella turns back around once the men are dressed.

"I think the mushrooms will be done now." Arella says. She takes her stick with the mushroom heads off the fire. She blows gently on the cooked mushrooms, steam drifting away from them. She takes a bite from one of them.

"What do they taste like?" Nashoba asks. Arella thinks for a second, chewing the mushroom carefully, taking in the taste.

"Like mouldy mud." She says. "A little gritty. But it's something."

"You're not making me want to try any." Mato laughs.

"It's either nasty mushrooms or nothing tonight. Your choice." Nootau laughs, taking his mushrooms from the fire. He bites into one. "Nope, she's right. They taste awful." They all laugh.

Once the mushrooms are all gone, reluctantly, Arella checks her clothes. "Nearly dry. They'll be fine in the morning." She yawns, sparking everyone else to yawn too.

"I think we should get some sleep." Nootau says, yawning. A roar sounds from outside the cave, the noise clearly far away, but echoing through the cave system. "Are you sure that thing can't get in here?"

"I hope so." Arella says. "If we struggled to get in here, then it shouldn't be able to make it through." Arella really hopes this is true, but she's not so sure. She takes one of the furs and curls up next to Maska. The others all take their places around the fire too, backs facing it to keep warm.

In the darkness, the sounds of the dying mares fill the air. The monster must have got them too in the dark. The sound is haunting, and Arella feels guilty for bringing the horses into the forest now. Without her, the horses would most likely still be alive, except for the one the dogs would have caught. Eventually the air falls silent. "Arella?" Nashoba's voice whispers.

"Yes?" She answers back.

"We will make it you know?" He says.

"I hope so."

Chapter 18

The morning light is streaming through the cave roof. Arella is the first to wake, soon followed by Maska. The air around them is silent, and the cave looks different in the light of the morning, more beautiful. The moss on the walls of the cave shimmer with greens and blues, water dripping on them keeping them alive. Small pools of water gather in places on the cave floor. Some of the pools are flowing into each other, and out of a small hole in the cave floor. The fire in the middle of the cave went out long ago, the cold is what woke her. Nashoba rolls over, opening his beautiful green eyes to look at Arella. "Morning." He says.

"Morning." Arella smiles. "We should get moving." She adds. "Wake the others?"

"Will do. Start packing everything up so we can move out fast?" Nashoba asks.

"Deal."

When everything is packed away, Arella, Nashoba, Maska, Mato and Nootau all depart the cave. Arella peeks her head out of the exit she found the night before, looking out to make sure the coast is safe. She looks out, but all she sees is more forest. Surrounded by the same pine trees that cover the rest of the forest. She listens for a minute, hearing nothing but the normal sounds of the forest. "I think we're okay to go." Arella says.

"Are you sure?" Nootau questions. "I don't want to go out there if that thing will be there."

"I can't hear it." Arella says. "And besides, it was on the other side of the cave. We should be okay." Arella still has an uneasy feeling about this forest. She wants to get out of there quickly, get away from the forest and this monster. She takes the first step outside, pulling her hood high to shield her eyes from the sun that beams down onto the forest floor below. Not much light is getting down to the floor, but it's enough to make Arella a little uncomfortable.

A magpie flies over head. "Morning Mr Magpie." Nashoba says. Arella smiles to herself. She was just about to say that. The magpie flies on past, not stopping. The ground in this part of the forest has very little grass or plants. With little light getting through, nothing much can grow. The bases of the pine trees here are wide, but with nothing much growing until head height. This makes moving through the forest fast.

"Did you hear that?" Nootau says.

"Hear what?" Nashoba says.

"I heard something." Nootau says. Arella looks around. She doesn't feel anything here, in the forest with her. There are no eyes watching her.

"Are you sure? I can't hear anything." She says. Just as she speaks, a rustle in a bush in front makes the, all stop. The bush rustles again. Arella takes her grathon in hand, holding one of the ends towards the bush. She steps forwards. A rabbit jumps out of the bush and runs in the opposite direction. Arella turns to look at Nootau. "A Rabbit." She starts laughing. "You were scared of a rabbit?"

"Oh come one." Nootau's a little annoyed at this. "It could have been the monster that chased us yesterday."

"In a bush that small?"

"You never know." They all start laughing now. The mood a lot lighter than it had been before.

"I'm going to climb a tree; see how far away from the mountains we are." Arella says. She drops her things to the ground and starts climbing the nearest pine. "Can you guys keep an eye on things down here? Let me know If anything happens?" He smiles his small smile, the one Arella feels is meant only for her. This lifts her spirits slightly.

"You know we will." Nashoba says. Arella starts climbing the tree, hand over foot, making sure she gets her footing right so not to slip. Her left shoulder is still a little sore, but she powers through it.

When she reaches the top, she is amazed by what she sees. They've not travelled far out of the way to the mountains, in fact they're pretty close to the foot of the mountains. Over the tops of the pine trees, Arella can see a blanket of fog. It hasn't penetrated the forest, but sits on top of the trees instead. It's a strange sight, but beautiful all the same. She climbs back down again to tell the men what she's seen.

"So we're not far away now then?" Mato asks.

"Not far from the base anyway. Then we have to climb the mountain." Nashoba says. "Wed better get going then. Do you think we will make it to the mountain today?" He asks Arella.

"We should do yeah." She says, pretty sure that they will.

Arella is suddenly aware that the forest is silent. "Can you hear that?" Arella asks.

"Hear what?" Nootau asks, listening hard.

"Shh." Arella shushes. They all listen hard for a minute. "Do you hear that?" Arella asks again.

"Hear what? I don't hear anything."

"Exactly." Arella says. "There's nothing. No noise at all. Where are all the birds?" The others think for a moment.

"Migrated for the winter?" Nootau asks hopefully.

"I don't think so." Arella says. "Let's just hope I'm wrong. Let's keep moving." A loud roar from behind them, a way off confirms Arella's fears. The monster is back. They all start moving faster, breaking into a slow run.

"I thought you said it could only come out at night." Nootau says to Arella.

"I said I saw it in the dark in a dream, I never said anything about it only coming out at night." The roar gets louder. "I can't believe this is happening" They break into a faster run, needing to keep out of the way of the horrible monster that has clearly now found them. "It must have picked up our scent."

"Keep moving." Nashoba says. "Maybe we can find another cave to hide in."

"I don't want to have to keep hiding in caves." Arella says, a little angry. "It might follow us all the way up the mountain if we do that. We have to get rid of it."

"What do you… suggest?" Nootau says, clearly out of breath already from the fast running.

"I don't know, but we're not going to outrun it." The ground underfoot is hard. The rain clearly didn't penetrate the canopy last night. With footsteps loud in the silent forest, there would be no hiding from the beast. It would sniff them out in seconds.

Another roar, this time louder, signals that the beast is closer to them now. Arella is the first to enter the clearing, the ground covered in soft meadow grass. The meadow is very long, and from the edge of the forest here, they can see the mountains. Their beautiful snow-capped tops clear against the deep blue sky. If they weren't running for their lives, Arella might stop to admire this view. "That's it! That's where we have to go!" Excitement washes over the group, quickly replaced by fear at the sound of the beasts roar.

A tree falls behind them, crashing to the ground. Arella turns to look into the forest where the noise came from. The others are still running, but stop when they hear the falling tree. Out of the darkness, still shrouded in the pine trees, the beast appears. It looks at Arella directly, her being the only one in view. A strange smile seems to stretch across its face, the flesh cracking a little as it does this. It blinks its red eyes at her, then opens its huge wolf mouth and roars. Arella notices its antlers are red with the dried blood of the horses. She feels sick looking at it, almost paralysed by fear. Images fill her mind again of her mare and the colt, their painful death cries echoing through her brain.

She turns around, and almost in slow motion, the monster starts charging at her. She looks over her shoulder again to see it even closer. She's had enough of this now, enough of being scared. She is coming up fast on Nashoba and the others in front. "Nashoba catch!" She shouts as she comes close. She takes her grathon in hand and throws it at him. He catches easily.

"Arella what are you doing?"

"Just trust me." She pulls her bow from around her chest and knocks an arrow. She turns fast, aims the arrow at the beast and fires. The arrow flies straight towards the beast, towards it's chest. It hits the beasts' chest, embedding its self-deep in the monster. It cries out in pain, but does not slow its pursuit. In fact, Arella might have made It angrier. She turns back to the men, all still running. "I don't think it worked." She shouts, panic in her purple eyes.

"Keep running." Nashoba shouts back. They keep moving, all as fast as their legs can move them. Maska at the front of the group, able to move much quicker on four legs. The beast is getting much closer, too close for comfort. Arella knocks another arrow, this time a bloodglass one. It's head glints in the sun as she pulls it back. She turns back around again and fires at the beast once more. This one catches the right leg of the monster. This catches it off guard, slowing it a little.

"Nice shot." Mato shouts.

"Don't congratulate me till we get away from that thing!" She shouts back. The beast stops to pull the arrow from its leg. It snaps the shaft as if it were a twig, then roars loud. It takes flight again, running faster than before towards Arella, its red eyes set on her.

"Arella?" Nashoba shouts back to her. "Arella you need to see this."

"What is it?"

"A problem." Nashoba shouts. She catches up, the beast not far behind. Arella sees the problem Nashoba was talking about. There is a canyon in the way, stopping them from going any further. At the bottom of the canyon, a raging river. "What do we do?" Arella thinks for a second, judging the gap.

"We have two choices." Arella says, looking back at the charging monster, too close to think straight. "We jump over, or we fight." Arella says.

"Jump?" Mato says, looking nervous. Arella draws another arrow and fires at the monster in an attempt to slow it. Time's up. It's upon them.

Arella snatchers her grathon back from Nashoba. "You guys get over. I'll hold it off."

"Not on your own!" Nashoba shouts.

"Just get over there Nashoba!" She shouts back, looking him directly in the eyes. The intensity at which she looks at him tells him she is not fooling around. "I'll draw it over there so you can get a run up, then you have to go."

This is complete insanity Arella knows it is. She has no idea what she is doing, or whether she will be able to draw the beasts atttention. With no time to think Arella quickly sidesteps with her gra - thon in one hand, her bow in the other, she begins waving her arms around. "Hey, ugly... Look at me!" Arella shouts. The monster is already looking at her, but she needs to keep it focused on her. She drops her grathon to the ground, kneels on the floor, knocks another arrow and fires it. The beast dodges it and flies directly at Arella. Now on all fours, saliva and death dripping from its jaws. She rolls out of the way, picking up her grathon as she does so. The beast lands with its head down, its antlers getting caught in a dead pine tree. It pulls its-self up on its legs, pulling at its head, trying to free its-self form the trunk of the tree it's stuck in.

This has bought the men enough time to make the jump. One by one they all take the run up, jumping the gap between the two bankings. They all make it, starting with Maska. Mato needs a little help to get up at the other side, breaking the rocky bank and slipping, nearly falling to his death, but they all make it. Arella lifts her grathon high into the air, intending to drive it into the beast, ending it forever. The monster pulls its-self free before she can land her killing blow. It falls into her, knocking Arella to the ground. With the wind knocked out of her, Arella is struggling to get up. She manages it, but only just before the monster can impale her with its antlers. The beast is furious now, foaming at the mouth, several of Arella's arrows sticking out of its grotesque body. From this close, she can see the creatures ribs and backbone. It's painfully hin, fingernails and toenails long and sharp.

She pulls the grathon up again, the monster speeding towards her. It comes right for her, head down, unable to see where it is going. Arella uses this to her advantage, diving once again to the side. The deer goes straight past her, and Arella is ready. She starts running, at full pelt towards the canyon. She makes it to the edge just as the beast does too. She jumps, aiming for the other side of the canyon. She makes it, her hands grabbing at the rocks on the other side. As she goes to pull herself up, the monster jumps. "Arella watch out!" Nashoba shouts. The next thing she knows; the monster has caught hold of her leg. She screams out in pain, the monster's claws scratching at her leg. It doesn't manage to hold on, and falls through the canyon. Its body hitting the rocks on the way down, cries of pain coming from it until it hits the water at the bottom.

Arella's grip fails her, the sweat from her own palms causing her to slip. First one hand, then the other. She cries out, knowing this is the end. Something grabs her from above, a warm hand. Arella looks up, the green eyes of Nashoba stare down at her. His strong hand holding her arm, saving her from certain death, the green eyed wolf hauls the white ghost back onto the land. "I've got you."

Chapter 19

Limping a little, but using her grathon for balance, Arella walks with Nashoba, Maska, Nootau and Mato. The forest on this side of the canyon can hardly be called a forest. The trees are very well spaced out, and they grow fairly small. Arella's wounded leg buckles from beneath her. Nashoba rushes to her side, helping get her up, then holding her, helping her to walk. "You're insane. Has anyone ever told you that?"

"Many times yeah." Arella laughs. "I got you away from it though didn't I?"

"True." Mato says. "But I think we'd all prefer if you'd done it without getting hurt."

"Ah well." Arella shrugs it off. "What's done is done and all that. Let's just get to the mountain."

"We need to find you some barrow berried too though, get that leg all healed up." Nootau says.

"That we do. Good luck finding..." Just as she says this. Masks trots up to her, twig with barrow berried in his mouth. He drops them at Arella's feet. "Bet you're feeling great now aren't you Maska?" She asks him. He just purrs at her. He then rubs himself on her leg, not the injured one though, showing her his affection. "Well thank you." She says.

"Look up." Nashoba says.

"What, what are we looking at?" Arella asks.

"The mountains. Nootau says. "We've made it to the mountains." They started walking uphill pretty soon after coming onto this side of the canyon without really realising it. Before they know it, more and more rocks have started cropping up around them. None of them were really paying attention to the landscape in front of them, all too tired to pay attention. Arella is feeling overjoyed. A cold breeze whispers through the air, bringing autumn leaves through with it, whirling them past Arella and towards the mountain. She looks up at the sky, silently thanking the spirits for the signs.

"Should we stop her for the night before going on to the mountain?" Arella asks.

"Not a bad idea, except one issue." Nashoba says, looking Arella in the eyes. She is mesmerised again by the green of his.

"What's that?" She asks, dreamy eyed.

"Food." He says. "We have no food."

"Maska can sort that out, can't you Maska?" Arella says to the auron cat in front of her. He walks over to Nootau and Mato, knocking into both of them as he pushes through them.

"What's he doing?" Mato says.

"I think he wants you to go with him." Arella laughs. "Maska, you could be nicer about asking." He meows at Arella in protest. "Go catch something nice for tea boy."

Nootau and Mato both follow Maska, not going too far away, still within sight of Arella and Nashoba on the sparse land. Nashoba helps Arella sit down on the ground. "So how do you apply the berries?" He asks.

"Oh it's okay." Arella says. "I can do it myself." Nashoba smiles at her.

"I want to help." He says. He removes Arella's boots, the one on her injured leg is removed slower than the other. He then peels her trousers back to reveal the scratches. The look deep. He takes a hand full of the berries and squashes them in his hands then begins to massage them into Arella's leg. She winces with the pain, but soldiers on through it. Once he has finished, Nashoba looks at Arella. He smiles at her. "Thank you."

"For what?" She says.

"For coming into my life." He leans forwards, closing his eyes and kissing Arella on the forehead. She smiles at this, his lips burning on her skin. Nashoba then moves away to start building a fire.

Arella watches from her place on the ground as Nashoba builds a fire, talking to himself as he does so, and as Nootau, Mato and Maska hunt for something close by. They come back with rabbits in hands. Four of them to be exact. "This cat is amazing at catching rabbits!" Mato says.

"Amazing!" Nootau echoes.

"We caught them, your time to skin and prepare them." Mato says to Nashoba.

"Fine. Not happy about it though." He says back. Arella laughs at the banter.

The sun has started to go down now, days getting even shorter. As the men cook the food, Arella sits staring at the mountain. She holds the red wolf Nashoba gave her in her hand, the heat of the wood alive against her skin. She's lost in her own world, staring at the snow on the mountain. Nashoba brings her back out of it with a fresh rabbit's leg, cooked to perfection right in front of her nose. Arella jumps out of her trance. "Thank you." She says, taking the leg.

"Speaking of legs." Nootau says, his mouth full of food. "Yours is looking much better." Arella examines her own leg.

"I guess it is yeah." She smiles, looking at Nashoba.

"So in the morning, we will leave here and head up the mountain." Nashoba says. "If we aim for the top of the mountain, there where the peek reaches the sky, I think we'll be in the right place."

"Sounds like a plan to me." Nootau says. He stretches and yawns. "Amazing how tired you get from running for your life."

"Think how I feel." Arella says.

"I think Maska must be the most tired." Mato argues.

"Yeah, and why's that?" Nashoba asks.

"He's already asleep." Mato laughs. It's true. The auron cat is snoring softly, laid on his back, his legs in the air.

"I think we need to follow his lead and go to sleep ourselves." Nashoba says.

"Not a bad idea." Arella says. She pulls her furs up closer to her neck, then lays down. The others all do the same.

Arella is suddenly aware of something on her hand. She looks down to find Nashoba's hand searching for hers in the darkness. She takes it, squeezing it tight. He squeezes back. Arella in certain she can see him smile. Tiredness washes over her as she watches the stars cross the cloudless sky.

Under the shadow of the mountain, with the stars above them in the open air, Arella, Maska, Nashoba, Nootau and Mato all sleep. Waiting for what tomorrow will bring, and the long treck up the mountain to see the mountain spirit.

Printed in Great Britain
by Amazon.co.uk, Ltd.,
Marston Gate.